Luis A. Aguilar Monsalve

In Search of Sister Edwina Marie

Luis A. Aguilar Monsalve

In Search of Sister Edwina Marie

A short novel

JustFiction Edition

Imprint

Any brand names and product names mentioned in this book are subject to trademark, brand or patent protection and are trademarks or registered trademarks of their respective holders. The use of brand names, product names, common names, trade names, product descriptions etc. even without a particular marking in this work is in no way to be construed to mean that such names may be regarded as unrestricted in respect of trademark and brand protection legislation and could thus be used by anyone.

Cover image: www.ingimage.com

Publisher:
JustFiction! Edition
is a trademark of
Dodo Books Indian Ocean Ltd. and OmniScriptum S.R.L publishing group

120 High Road, East Finchley, London, N2 9ED, United Kingdom
Str. Armeneasca 28/1, office 1, Chisinau MD-2012, Republic of Moldova, Europe
Printed at: see last page
ISBN: 978-620-0-10700-8

Luis A. Aguilar Monsalve

In Search of Sister Edwina Marie

(A short novel)

ONE

The silence of the night hides in the ancient cloister, and in their cells, the nuns are rapt in an elusive sleep. Beneath a massive wooden crucifix and images of saints with angelic gazes that hang on the wall over each of the beds' headboards, they rest, accompanied by their rosaries. They dream about remote worlds with desolated mangers and their own secret anguishes, sometimes moaning in suspense or encircled by breaths of guilt of no recognizable sources. They wait for the first hour of dawn, and with the jarring sound of the bell, they swiftly leave their beds to kneel on the tiled floor. In haste, they bless themselves as if they want to slice the air and find in the unknowable the strength not to falter. Every one will press her hands together, and she will touch her rough lips. Perhaps someone will recall a kiss and the sweetness of a gentle act, and then the daily prayers will start. Others, with hands clasped in prayer, will place fingertips on shy lips, and the dream will be confined to obscurity. One yawn will be enough to feel the shower of frost penetrating like glass pins while far off, the beseeching echo of the lost flock of sheep will be heard.

A keen voice emanates from the center of the *Holy Mary, conceived without sin,* and this first invocation seems to arise from aural nails hammered into it in a remote time. *Our Father, who art in heaven, hallowed be thy name. Thy kingdom come, thy will be done on earth as it is in heaven. Give us this day our daily bread; and forgive us our trespasses as we forgive those who trespass against us; and lead us not into temptation, but deliver us from evil. Amen.*

Hail Mary, full of grace, the Lord is with thee. Blessed art thou among women, and blessed is the fruit of thy womb, Jesus. Holy Mary, Mother of God, pray for us sinners, now and at the hour of our death. Amen.

Glory be to the Father, and to the Son, and to the Holy Spirit. As it was in the beginning, is now, and ever shall be, world without end. Amen.

The cells, pervaded with poverty, austerity, and little from the world beyond them, receive the divine whisper. No dullness is in these prayers. One and all experience the union with the Beloved. They leave the dream aside and concentrate on a bittersweet meditation. A delicate, stubborn residue lingers, serving as a mythical bulge, a cushion of remembrance that the human being, blessed or not, is an animal with dark instincts. Within seconds, they feel saturated with internal joy sheltered by faith and their connection solely to God. In the following moment, they are overcome with a manifold somberness because they understand that they have exempted themselves from all human relationships; their situation is unique and spiritual. The sun smears while entering and playing through the optical gash of an agonic moon that is showing the vestiges of the night in its furious charge.

The chapel glimmers from the dense candlelight, and a golden splendor appeases the early morning. Outside the chapel, the scene is dressed in blackish blue, and inside, pecks a contemplative, tepid, and sublime air. The candles burn at a tortuous pace, preparing the entrance for the nuns, who, in every motion of their slow promenade, reflect about sacred uncertainties, virtuous invocations, and fervent feelings. Gathered, the religious women proceed in a double line to the presbytery.

In the flickering shadows at the altar, the novices stand still, releasing the scapulars enfolded in their hands, and join their palms together in prayer. Closing their eyes, they bow with modesty, they kneel, they lie down on the floor, and with open arms, they each form a perfect cross of subjection. In silence, they communicate with the Lord. They all give thanks for one more day of life, they ask for forgiveness of their sins, and they plead for the wellbeing of all.

3

The nuns in their black habits, watching from a distance behind, simulate uneven mountain peaks on any corner of any mountain range, but these lack the white cold and compact summits of those. Little by little, the twenty-one women, whose faces are shining with an inner peace, can be distinguished. They are united with God in an intimate and serene dialogue. More than one will caress the silver ring and will acknowledge again that she is His wife forever, which always sounds so exclusive, so destined, and so invulnerable. The beads in their hands travel breadths in the midst of bits of supplications, daily devotions, and smiles lost in the dreariness beyond the candle flames.

Dominating the center of the chapel is an enormous crucifix, and from the effects of the trembling light, it seems to perspire in the absence of suffering and to passively accept its incomparable mission. Because it is varnished in red, His body appears to exude a thick blood that is throbbing with more intensity at the rib cage and at the wide forehead crowned with stabbing thorns. The only incongruity in this tremendous, pathetic picture is the harbor of Christ's eyes, imbued with forgiveness, compassion, and hope.

With reticence, the Mother Superior, an elderly woman with a grooved complexion and naturally graceful bearing, positions herself in front of the sanctuary and hides her long and thin hands. The religious arrange themselves in the benches to pray as one, starting as a family their first spiritual nourishment and first action of a today already broken by a cryptic, dying today, by a future with nothing requested or desired.

Each one of them has the necessary time to enter into contact with her Owner and to pursue a Pio ambience of mysticism and peace that cannot be found outside, where selfishness, fear, ambiguity, and scarcity are a tempest and a torment. The Mother Superior leads in praying the rosary, and they reply in choir until the five mysteries are finished. They then begin the daily prayers with the consecutive meditations, the canticles in honor of Jesus, the Virgin Mary, and the Holy Spirit.

TWO

"My own, again all alone and so distant. . . . You don't want to answer me, dear? Or perhaps you haven't heard me."

"Yes, I heard you, Mother. I am not alone, I am with God. Can anyone be distant when the Lord is with us?"

"Amanda, you have thoughts as if you are an expert in Church doctrine."

The child smiled with reserve and continued looking through the window at the expanse of flamboyant greens and blues. Her parents' unpretentious house had been there for many years. It was constructed by her great-grandparents, whom she had never met. She was the beneficiary of unspoken testimonials to many past generations. Her mother, Griselda, the only daughter, was born there. She was mischievous and teasing and would cry over anything. She grew up in the country and went to school reluctantly. Sunday mornings would particularly annoy her because of the monotony of the catechism and the Mass, which was officiated by Father Manuel, an aging priest with an impulsive nature but who was popular. The child's parents worked in the fields and would go to the town only when it was necessary.

Griselda became a teenager and was barely eighteen years old when she fell in love with Cipriano. She could not think of anything but him. The young man, at nineteen years old, was a troublemaker and conceited and in charge of everything that crossed his path. As was expected, his future in-laws did not like him, but he ignored their treatment of him. He was kind, and they eventually approved of him.

One April afternoon, Cipriano had presented himself at Griselda's house, but he did not have with him the hares he regularly brought her parents. He astounded everyone by asking for Griselda's hand in marriage. He broke as many protocols for the courtship and engagement rituals as possible. There was no time to waste. Silliness, he called any interference with his plans or way of life. He would use this term to pass as an educated man. However, in him was an extensive repertory of swear words for which Father Manuel told him to wash his mouth out with soap made of harsh ingredients.

On this day, he was clad in a brown, light wool jacket, a white cotton shirt, snug blue trousers, and mid-calf, straw-colored chamois boots. Crossing his chest was a thick, unhardened leather strap, and from it hung a thin bag that rested at his left waistline. His wing hat matched his boots. He sat down in the closest chair to the door. With a determined flourish, he freed his long hair, and it fell until it grazed his shoulders. In his usual style, he wore his abundant, black, curly hair pulled back tight behind his ears. He managed himself with confidence, to the astonishment of everyone who was subjected to his speech. His spiel defied any conventions in this case. He did not consider Griselda's reaction because he had not even told her about his intentions. The parents and daughter were stunned and did not rush to comment about his proposal. They were paralyzed, vaguely conscious that the solitary motion was beyond the window: the Jacaranda branches swinging steadily and slowly over the sheet of violets, which the mid-afternoon was painting an inconceivable blue.

The patriarch, Don Secundino, finally arose after clearing his throat and moving his eyes in many directions. He extended his lips from one side to the other, wetting them, as if with these gestures and some saturation, he would find the aid to give a certain logical quality to a matter as desperate as the one that was growing. How was it plausible that he, the oldest and the owner of the house, would allow a younger person to monopolize the conversation to the stage of dictating to all of them! He cleared his throat again, frowned, and fixed his honey pupils on the jet black eyes of this daring but immature man. Crossing his arms behind his back with vigor, he stood before Cipriano and confronted his audacity with a voice of such might that the women slumped imperceptibly lower into the chairs that partitioned the modest living room from the dining room.

"Wedding, matrimony, hey!" he said, biting every word and polishing them so they would fall with clarity on naïve minds and hearts. He continued with the same authoritarian tone. "Do you suppose that making a home is entirely as easy as opening your big mouth, to sit with your legs spread apart—a sign of a bad education—" He was staring at Cipriano's groin with absolute dismay. "And then to venture to ask for the hand of a sweet, innocent, and diligent creature, my daughter, in marriage? Well, no, mister, I will not permit an anticipated misfortune to happen to this poor small child, who is not familiar with the vile world—" He looked at his daughter with compassion, and in the meantime, she was screaming on the inside that, yes, she would marry him, that she did not love him, instead, she adored him, and which thought would cause her father, if he knew, to be even more furious because one just adores God and not any mortal being.

Cipriano seized the opportunity and quickly included his opinion. "Don Secundino." he said with neither wariness nor insolence, "we love each other, and she and I would be miserable if we couldn't be together. I got an additional job at Don Nicolás's estates besides the work I do with my father every morning and part of every afternoon, and he will give us the shack to live in until I can build a house on my land." He emphasized his last words with firmness and pride. "I will take Griselda and her mother there so they can organize everything to Griselda's liking. For me, I don't care. I am not interested in women's affairs."

He was talking with so much command and conviction that Don Secundino was filling with anger and the desire to strike him, but he restrained himself because of propriety and the way Griselda was looking at Cipriano. Cipriano finished speaking, and he crossed his legs in the manner of an aristocratic man. At this, Don Secundino became more irate than ever, retorted with the same antagonism as he had before, and having surpassed his patience, tossed him out of the house. As Cipriano sauntered off, Griselda—dressed in a flowery skirt and a pearl-colored, short-sleeved blouse, but barefoot—reminded him that she loved him and would wait for him forever. She was fainting as her mother, Doña Rosario, reached for her and lowered her head onto her right leg. She asked her husband to bring wet towels to lay on their daughter's flushed face that was showing too soon a future of suffering. The father recovered somewhat from his anemic state and marched off to bring what she had requested.

THREE

It was a Saturday, and the sun was hitting the town's reddish roofs. The many-colored facades of the houses were streaked with the reflected light reaching them, imitating, from a distance, noisy ghosts. The streets' paving stones had been crippled by the traffic over time. The

8

main route would pick up the flurry of vehicles, businessmen, itinerant traders, and peasants with their animals and birds heading to the market. One or another outsider who wanted to rest on one of the stone benches would cross over the river that divided the valley from the town. Once in a while, the small children would run along the canal banks to observe how a mother goose would plunge into the abysm, and the goslings, desperate with loneliness, would tumble forward and also land in the water. Then, safe with their mother, they would flap their tiny tails. The church and the nuns' convent could be identified by the drab brick of the building. The chiming of the bell in the tower resonated throughout the fresh air and pastoral countryside, echoing a remote era that could never reappear, and unremittingly attended all the neighborhood activities beside the foot of the mountain. No one could prevent assimilating the sound of the ancestral music, constant and clear.

Each one of the religious women who will enter the convent should reflect that when she gives herself to the Lord, she would sacrifice her life for a better one.

Amanda, Cipriano and Griselda's daughter, has returned to her house, and from her bedchamber, she looks out a small window that oversees the vast horizon broken by the clouds. A little anxious, she passes her right hand back and forth over the pearl necklace that her mother gave her on her fifteenth birthday. It is as though she wants to use it like the rosary that is in the pocket of her jacket or that she wants to feel it as the object it is, jewelry.

I notice in her deportment a hesitancy, a slight stagger of a young woman's indecision. I start to be interested and to understand her.

She wears a navy blue, tailored suit that falls past three-quarters of her legs, and black, low heel shoes. She is slender, almost too thin. She smiles. But even though her smile is tender, it is sad. It is one that invites respect and affection. She strokes the ring that her grandparents gave her for her first communion. She remembers taking it a couple times to the jewelry shop to have it repaired. She slides it around and then off her thin finger and sets it on top of her Kempis beside the crucifix that someone brought to the house and that she moved to her bedroom after no one reclaimed it. She turns her attention again to the necklace. Without delay, she removes it, and when it is in her right hand, she examines it, the fingers of her left hand walking through it. She touches it to her nose and then to her lips, and a miniscule tear stains a deep green eye. She lays it on the opposite side of the book of prayers. Her equanimity is enviable. She glances at the landscape once more and closes the window. She surveys her bedroom: the bookshelf, the dresser that she has had since she was twelve years old, the single bed, the bench upholstered in pale pink with wildflower buttons, and the framed mirror made by her father. She blinks but does not smile. She takes her delicate hat from one of the chairs, places it upon her head, and secures it with a black pin. She picks up her suitcases and walks out of the room that has belonged to her for nineteen years.

Her mother and father wait for her downstairs. Both pretend to be tranquil and reconciled, which is far from their genuine state of mind. Amanda pauses on one of the top steps of the staircase. She is momentarily detained by guilt but composes herself hurriedly, thinking that if she would leave her home to set up another one, it would be a similar trial for her parents. She forces a smile that is generous so that it is more noticeable. She quickly descends and hugs her mother with all the energy she can summon. Griselda does not speak a word, and her and Cipriano's breathing is shallow.

"Are you ready?" Cipriano asks.

"Yes."

"Your hat is crooked."

"I tried to put it on without using the mirror."

A hint of resentment gleams in her eyes. She tries not to think about what will happen within the day, that she has committed to the Almighty. Cipriano raises his hands and straightens the hat by shifting it a few inches to its right.

"Now, it looks nice. I like that.'

"I am not expecting my grandparents. They told me that they wouldn't be here today. We said goodbye last Wednesday."

"Yes, your mother told me."

Griselda goes to Amanda. She does not want to part with her daughter, and she can't control her weeping.

"My Amanda! If for any reason you stop feeling what you feel right now, this is your home, and as long as your father and I live—" Her voice fades away. She resumes in a few seconds. "You always will have a place here. May God bless you and always be with you."

"Mother, I am leaving because I am sure that God has planned a mission for me on earth. I am also leaving because I want to be with Him for eternity. But that does not mean that I could ever love you less."

Her mother, repressing unbearable sorrow over her loss, blesses her. Amanda kisses her hands, hugs her, and retrieves her luggage. Cipriano raises his left arm and pulls her to his side. They pass through the door, and he closes it.

In the yard, Maite, her best friend from school, is waiting for her. She gives her a gardenia. Amanda smells it. She smiles and gives it back. They embrace each other. A discussion between them would be contrived. She murmurs next to her ear, "Take care of them for me." And she releases her, trying to contain the tears that are the sum of all her emotions accumulated in many days of conformity and denial.

"Let's go, Child."

They enter the taxi for the trip to the convent. Each future novice arrives at the church's atrium with one of her parents. The bells sound faster. Cipriano and Amanda get out of the car. He carries her luggage, and she holds on to his arm as she used to do when he picked her up at the end of the school day.

"I accept all the changes in you, but that you will be governed and will depend on a bell, I do not believe. You are going to suffer." And looking at the church, he persists, "Your personal life will end after you climb these stairs into this huge building."

She only smiles. A dog, thinned by malnutrition caused by neglect, approaches them with its tongue out. It sniffs, inspects them with good will, perhaps advocating a life it does not understand, shakes its tail, and runs down the street, receding beyond people's sight and sighs.

"I better go alone, Father." With meekness, she removes his arm.

"I brought you here, why be alone? You have my blessing and your mother's. I would never leave you, especially today when you are at a crossroad. If, for any reason, the life you want, that you are about to start, is not for you, there is no shame in abandoning it and returning to what is yours."

She does not defend her decision but simply looks at him with devotion. "Let's continue," he says in a robust voice and with no hesitation. He clutches her arm, and she allows him to guide her as she turns her face toward the cobbled wall. At the entrance door, she stops, glances back at the streets behind her, then at her father, and smiles once more. They let a future novice, who is with her mother, step in front of them and into the building, and they follow.

FOUR

The chill of autumn has stopped being felt temporarily in the apse of the building. There are nine applicants, all of them in dark coats and hats. They enter with the parents, and they chat about their last concerns before locking themselves away for a life of contemplation, seclusion, and prayer. *Kyrie Christe Eleison* music from the convent chapel surrounds them. The baroque architecture of the enclosure stands like a grotesque face thrown by chance from hands that abused the adornments Curved lines emphasize a complex ornamentation. All the candidates have a self-possession that surprise all of us who look from the outside and do not understand what would be The Call.

A smooth squeak of an antiquated door is suddenly heard as it opens. All of them direct their eyes to where it is strategically fitted into the left-hand wall. Two nuns walk through the doorway. One is the postulants' director, Sister Maria Esther del Niño Jesus, and the other is Sister Josefina de los Angeles, who keeps the convent's accounts and collects all the dowries. The two greet everyone with courtesy and natural smiles; however, something dispassionate is evident on the lips of these women who have found a path that has accustomed them to a behavior beyond anything that is ordinary. To demonstrate that they as yet have some sociability and they haven't forgotten how a relationship is between civilized people, they mingle with the participants. They recognize the presence of a woman with a child in her arms, and they smile

13

more affably even though one of the requirements has been broken: They should be there with only one person, preferably a parent, per applicant.

"Good afternoon."

"Good afternoon, Your Reverences," Cipriano says.

Sister Maria Esther leans toward Amanda and affects kissing her on the side of each of her cheeks. Sister Josefina stands rigidly behind them and limits herself to a smile, but this time, she has a warm look.

"We find ourselves so proud of our Amanda."

"That is what I hope for, and I will always be."

"She has a good disposition, and we like her very much."

"Thank you, Mother. We will miss her in a way you cannot imagine."

"We will take good care of her."

"Thank you again, Mother."

The religious move away from him and engage in a decorous conversation with the other families. Sister Josefina returns, and Cipriano gives her a closed envelope containing the donation. After receiving it, she retires to continue her chores. She has not said a word; her one instrument of communication is the smile.

"How can you live without speaking? It is not human."

"Father, one gets used to everything, especially if the sacrifice one does is in the name of the Lord."

Cipriano places his strong hands on his daughter's slim arms. For a moment, they do not say anything. The eyes carry an intimate discourse in a restructured version of a family. His daughter is definitely going away from home. It is a reality that he did not comprehend completely until now. He is short of breath; the air has become drier, more vicious. He is losing his daughter, and even as noble as the convent is, this one is about to swallow his child. He gives her his blessing, kisses her forehead, and departs with quick steps. Amanda stays, watching him leave, and there is no smile, merely a cast of resignation. Soon, tears are in her eyes Her father disappears.

The other applicants also break away from the mothers and fathers and advance to the staircase. They have readily adopted serenity and submissiveness. Their actions are precise, and one would say that even their movements meditate on what they are doing and the marks they have left on each platform. Amanda is the last one to go up the stairs. She realizes her desire to be a nun will be a reality. She sees the space that separates the voracious world from the mystical cloister of prayer and sacrifice. Her thoughts are with her parents and the smell of home. Why is it so hard to be happy? The tears finally splash onto her cheeks, and her hand dries them. Sister Maria Esther, standing at the threshold, cheers her up with a sympathetic look. Amanda smiles again with diffidence. She pushes the door, and it gradually opens, letting out a rumbling proclamation as if it were the introduction to an expressive, but unfathomable, toast.

In a large, well-lighted room, the applicants remove their clothing. Amanda takes off her navy blue suit and white silk blouse, along with the silk stockings and the leather shoes, and packs them into a suitcase that is labeled with her name. At once, each sister grabs a black skirt, a shirt of the same color, and a white collar. They dress, last of all pulling on black muslin socks and worn, black leather shoes that match the bland, new garb. A prodigious crucifix suffused with pain, probably a reproduction of an ultramarine Legarda, one speculates, welcomes them. From the highest point of one wall, the Dying considers the women who have consented to his call. At the other side, a Murillo's Virgin greets them. They proceed to a polished walnut table, on which rest the black veils and capes. The veils will be fixed to the tops of their foreheads and will fall to their backs, and the capes will drape them from their shoulders to their waistlines. Some of them have short haircuts, some wear their hair up in buns, and others have tastefully long hair or luxuriant braids that curl down to the ends of their hair. They are prepared for their new life.

Sister Maria Esther is at the head of the table and gives them the congratulatory message. She has an attitude of marbled elegance, not offensive, but, rather, a metallic detachment that is enviable. All of them receive this impression, and the postulants admire this nun who one day found herself in the same position as they are in now. By instinct or practice, she feigns some concern, and the young women acknowledge the first change: This realm is impersonal, and the only relationship that should exist is the one with God.

"Sisters, you have just left your relatives and have entered our institution that serves Our Lord. The rule is fundamental and very effective, as you know: We prepare for a better life in the company of our Creator. Besides the mandatory vows in the religious life—chastity, obedience, and poverty—we have the vow of silence. We always bear in mind that we should get rid of all our habits and develop new ones, for example, how to put on our veils without mirrors and to keep our hands covered. You shall go out only when a chore requires you to be outside.

"I should ask all your attention to the vow of silence, for you should only talk when a superior addresses you. Among you shall be no communication. The first week will be very difficult, and many of you will revert to the habit of talking. Remember that the problem is not to incur fault. Immediately, you should be asking for forgiveness of God, and the other applicant should not answer. Resist always the company of others. Physical contact should never exist, and never long for something unnecessary for one. Make sacrifices constantly and offer them to our Beloved. We have to learn how to be by ourselves but full of the presence of our Savior. We should pray continuously in silence, and we should look for daily communication with Him. We should not call attention to ourselves. We should always do well. We strive to do everything gently and quietly. We should walk by the wall and with our eyes down in the sign of meditation. Now we will go to the chapel to listen to Mother Superior, to whom we should love and obey without questioning. She represents the Almighty in our convent. Afterward, we will pray the night prayers."

Formed in two rows, they listen intently. They are not frightened of the transition demanded of them. Sister Maria Esther pulls out a hefty key from her pocket and opens the door. With expectant faces, they file into the narrow corridor and enjoin themselves to pray silently. Encompassing them is music from a Venetian organ played by an elderly religious, the instrumental *In Paradisum Angeli*. In the chapel, on knees and with hands in arches, they lay their foreheads upon the uppermost back edges of the wooden benches before them. Together, they now utter their prayers.

"Hail Mary, most pure."

"Conceived without sin."

The nuns who already have some years in the ambience intone the Gregorian chants, and they end with Schubert's *Hail Mary*. The Mother Superior sits on a rustic wooden chair in front of the altar. Covered in black except for a white wimple that protects most of her forehead, only her face can be seen. Tired-looking, blue eyes stand out, but they are docile eyes. The nose is sharp and angular, and the thin lips conceal an irregular, yellowish denture.

"My daughters, until today I haven't met you, but from this instant, with the permission of our Lord, your destiny will be connected to my prayers and decisions, which you will have to take for your everyday progress. Your salvation, your ministry, your wishes are in my hands.

17

which are the hands of our Creator, humbly accepted by me for your success and reward in our holy community. Today, you have abandoned, by your own choice, the world where we were born. None of you have been coerced to be here. The commencement of anything is harsh, uncertain, and murky. But with prayer, the daily prayer of the *Lauds* and *Vespers*, awaiting the arrival of *Angelus*, the chores, and the strict obedience to your vocation, you will be free, and your values will change with the help of this poor woman, who is but a thorn in the crown of our Redeemer. Today, it will seem very difficult to live here, but with time—and time erases everything, my daughters—you will achieve what you now aspire to. I guarantee a peace that you will obtain only inside these walls. Your lives, which are for all, will be of happiness but not the one you are accustomed to. I will teach you how to live to die, that is, to always stay with our Lord Jesus Christ."

Two by two, they advance to the center of the chapel, they kneel, and they lie down on the floor, their arms serving as cushions where they support their foreheads.

"My daughters, now that you are here, what do you ask for?"

"We ask to be admitted, and we are looking for salvation for the world with the help of God, the help of Your Reverence, and the sisters who are in charge of our preparation," they answer in unison.

"If this is your desire, you are welcome."

FIVE

After he leaves the convent, Cipriano stops in the middle of the square. A sporadic spatter of rain is sufficiently irritating to alter the normal rhythm of the inhabitants. There is a smell of wetland and flowers blooming. He looks back and appraises the cloister and the church with its illuminated dome in all its physical and mental vastness. It is so close to him, and, nevertheless, it is so remote. . . . He has left his child locked up, as is her one request, in a bricked cemetery that weaves her into an incomprehensible and unnatural world. He cannot do a thing to change that, to pull his child out of this deceitful hole. At a standstill, he breathes and straightens his hat. It slips to his right, and he sinks his hands into the pockets of his suit and gulps the air and walks on. Passing through his mind are a thousand and one disconnected ideas. His bad mood is back again. His powerlessness tortures him to an agony that dries his throat, but breaths of the humid air relieve it a little. Near the bridge, he remembers where he got out of the car with Amanda, stealing several seconds with her from the infamous fate that seized her and would entomb her in a precarious future. . . . *I accept all the changes in you. But that your life will be governed and will depend on a bell, I do not believe. You will suffer, my child. . . . You will suffer, my child. . . . You will suffer, my child. . . .*

He doesn't speak to anybody and examines his deplorable circumstance more than once. Perhaps someone will understand him, but no one will be capable of feeling what he is now, maybe the most disastrous moment in his life. To lose a daughter forever is a pain not comparable to anything. *Do not tell me because she is in a convent that she is alive. I just buried her. I just failed her.*

He enters Don Anselmo's bakery and finds a loaf of French bread, a bottle of natural yogurt, and some strawberries. He doesn't buy the black jam that his only child loves so much, but he remembers Griselda and adds a bottle of heavy cream. He pays cash but neglects to pick up the change.

"Don Cipriano, your change."

He doesn't hear, but with fast steps, he departs with the bread under his right arm. He wants to be home to sit in his armchair, close his eyes, and forget everything. *I just got older.* He does not notice a loose tile, and he falls to the street. He bumps his left ear. It bleeds, and he feels a swelling. Free from the shock and again on his feet, he pulls out a handkerchief from his back pocket to blot the wound, and a red stain appears on it. He tucks it away. He lifts the bottle and notes that it is not cracked, and he breathes more calmly. His wife will enjoy life in the middle of sadness, and he will have to strain to continue an existence that has been cut short. The bread is still in one piece but has a film of dust; he wipes it off and pins it beneath his elbow again. Nothing has happened to the strawberries and the yogurt.

A flock of sheep comes down the main street, the youthful shepherd humming a bucolic melody. He sees them in shadows. He recognizes an elderly man slowly herding a considerable number of geese and talking to himself. He has a walking cane, and every so often, he uses it to keep the birds together. The men greet each other. He wants to go home quickly. He imagines Griselda sobbing for their daughter, and he wants to be there. . . . *I am leaving because I am sure God has me signed up for a mission in this world. I am leaving because I want to be with Him for all eternity.* . . .

He has the urge to curse, but he controls himself and mentally invokes the Holy Trinity. Rain evolves from the drizzles. He is getting wet, and he begins to sneeze. He arrives at his house and discovers Griselda, lost in thought, sitting in the wicker rocking chair that she bought a few weeks ago from the neighbor who was moving from the area.

"You are soaked," she says, standing up. "What is wrong with your ear?"

"Nothing, nothing. It is scarcely a scratch. Can you bring me a warm tea with lemon?" He takes off his hat and coat.

"I prepared it when the rain started."

He nods his head with appreciation, and he tries to smile. Griselda follows him to the kitchen, where he shows her the groceries he bought. Neither of them wants to talk about Amanda.

Finally, the warm drink soothes him, and he says, "I left her well. She is happy. Sister Maria Esther del Niño Jesús seems to like her a lot. She will help her if she needs anything."

"Do not believe that. They are there to suffer, to pray for us, and to watch out for themselves. Life on this earth hinders them. They say that they live to die. They will not do a thing to help our daughter."

She covers her face with the end of the apron and cries bitterly. Cipriano tries to comfort her by taking her in his arms. He holds her firmly, and the inevitable tears fall down his face. He makes sure that his wife does not see or feel them. He is successful. When he is in the dining room, he slices a piece of bread, dips it in the cream, and eats it. He prepares a plate of strawberries for Griselda and serves her. She does not want to eat, but with a little encouragement, she does. Afterward, she stands up and finishes preparing the supper. He retreats to the living room, turns on the record player, and plays one record repeatedly. The one he chose was *Perfidia*. He stretches out in his favorite chair and closes his eyes. *Mujer si puedes tú con Dios hablar, pregúntale si yo alguna vez, te he dejado de adorar. . . .* From a distance, the warble of a sparrow can be heard, the rain has stopped, and a celestial brightness floods the region.

Damn it! I am not going to lose Griselda just because those old people think I do not deserve her. No, sir! I will not find an extra job. I will enroll in night classes, and I will get my degree. I will graduate, and afterward, I will study more to seek a better profession. Griselda has to see my point of view and support me. First, I have to talk to my father. Damn, that will be hard. Why do people intrude in somebody else's business?

"Father, I want to talk to you."

"Ah, what are you saying, Son? I just came in, and if we don't get rain soon, the harvest will be deplorable."

Don Ramón brushes off his clothes, picks up his pipe, lights it and puffs on it, and settles into his chair. "What were you saying?" he asks as he smokes the cheap, sugary tobacco.

"I have to talk to you," he says with awkwardness and trepidation but, most of all, hiding discouragement because he will no doubt disappoint his father, who expects a lot from him. "I decided not to accept the extra job at Don Nicolas's estate. With your permission, I want to take classes at night in the high school. I want to have a profession. I want to be someone in life, like Father Manuel says. Will you support me?"

Don Ramón smokes, his eyes fixed on his son's face. He coughs and says, "I talked with the priest the other day. He called me. He has put in your head that you can and should go to school. Your generation is not like ours, that I should tie you to this land that gives us life. Maybe he is right. I have seen many changes in my days, and there will be more that will come, and they are not pleasant, no, sir. It will bring us sorrow and more poverty. What about your marriage? Have you already forgotten Griselda, Mr. Scholar?"

"No, Father, exactly because I am thinking of her and our future, I want to take a risk and try something new. I love this land like you do, but I want a different future for myself. I want

22

options. I hate to tolerate my future as it comes just because it's not written like that. I wasn't a bad student when I was in school."

"Neither were you good."

"True, Father, but now I can't afford to be an average student because I have to mold my future."

"'To mold my future.' Prove it. Your tongue is already getting sharper, and you are a lawyer good for nothing."

Cipriano smiles. He moves closer to his father. As he used to do when he was a child, Don Ramón wraps his arms around him and holds him for a while. What does the passing of time matter when you have what is yours near you or you have recovered it? He grasps his son's face in his rough hands, regards him with love, and kisses his wide forehead. Cipriano has his father's approbation, and now no obstacle impedes him, he is sure.

Don Ramón anticipated the conversation. "I knew it would require a change in plans, and that you were ready for that. It could be that they will call you to the army, and you will have to serve your country. You have my blessing. But you haven't answered my question about Griselda." He separates himself from his son with gentleness.

"I have to marry her because I love her. I can't stop thinking about her for one minute. She is needed more than the air I breathe." He once heard this last sentence at some time in some impressive place, but now he feels it.

"Your mother used to believe that. Despite the years she hasn't been with us, I think about her every day. And every day, I need her. And you were twenty months old when she turned away from us. You cannot miss her."

23

His son does not reply to this. Cipriano sees how Don Ramón's countenance changes, becoming impassive, with an enigmatic agenda. The scene that he has recorded in his memory flashes through his mind: On the porch bench, to the right side and letting all the detachment be observed and dispersed, sometimes becoming limitless, Don Ramón can be found sitting with his left leg crossed over the other one, the right arm extended on the back of the seat, looking down. It is as though he is leaving space for Doña Jacinta to be close to him and in his state, she is. On many occasions, Don Ramón shakes his head, and with a spiteful expression, curls into the shadows. *Where and with whom are you, Jacinta?*

And you,

who knows where you have been,

who knows what adventures you have, how far you are from me. . . .

The air is announcing the coming of fall. Cipriano arrives at the school and registers for night classes to complete high school. He will have to finish in twenty-four months, but if he dedicates two Saturdays a month to attending the program, he can graduate in a year and a half. He whistles. With his hands in his pockets, he kicks the smaller stones he stumbles across, and when he manages to hit one with another, he raises his arms and jumps, breaking into a broad smile. To prevent a mishap, he helps a woman with a little boy in her arms cross a ditch. It is not hard to find happiness, he concludes.

The night dominates, and the lights and the antique lamps illuminate as though a baton is awakening and aligning them. At Griselda's house, he kisses her with urgency until she pulls away from him because she never welcomed him with so much intimacy.

"My God, Cipriano, what is with you?"

He smiles, and he displays total calmness and confidence.

"Nothing, nothing is going on with me, but also all is going on. '

"What did you drink?"

"Nothing, but I have drunk everything."

"Cipriano, I don't understand. You aren't drunk, but you're scaring me."

He takes her in his arms again, and not relinquishing an almost childish grin, he kisses her with tenderness. She responds with passion, and he whispers in her ear, "Tomorrow, we will get married. I want you to trust in it, memorize it, and make it yours. From now on, your life and mine are one."

"Good."

She has no difficulty agreeing to his wish because she knows he would not harm her and that he needs her now and always.

"Have you talked with Father Manuel?"

"I will, I will talk to him. You and I are old enough. We will go to the registry office. I will come for you at nine-thirty, and we will be there minutes before they open. Father Manuel will tell your parents and my father the news. If they want to come, they are welcome. I won't have any problem with my father. Oh! Don't tell them anything."

"No. Better, we will meet there. I don't want them to stop me. I don't want any confrontation. I do not want to lose you. I won't tell them."

The shed, in the back part of the La Bruyére's house, was an outdated barn. They rented it and remodeled it to have a dining room, an efficiency kitchen on the right, and on the left, a bedroom with a bathroom. It fascinated Griselda. The two families helped furnish it with the essentials, and she decorated it. She found a job at Don Lorenzo's corner store. She worked

Monday through Friday, from eight to noon and from four to six in the afternoons. She persuaded them not to call her in on Saturdays. Cipriano was working tirelessly with Don Ramón, and everything they didn't consume, they sold at the market. They also began selling to his wife's boss at a reduced price. After being married two months, and becoming accustomed—or, better, having adapted—to each other, both were convinced that marriage had been the correct choice. They were happy, and it would last until death.

The studies weren't easy for him. He met Juan José Oliveira, who had less difficulty. He was nineteen years old, like Cipriano. They became the best of friends and studied together. Juan José was an excellent teacher. Griselda learned how to cook better, she maintained a clean and orderly house, and she even found time to take care of her father-in-law, who had meals with them. When he invited them to move in with him, they declined. At the end of the first year of studies, Cipriano finished his exams with outstanding scores. With his transcript, he ran to his father's home, and they called Griselda.

"What happened? What are you doing? What are you giving me?"

"Look at it, I passed and with good grades."

"And Juan José?" Griselda asked.

"He had very high grades also," he said with unequivocal pleasure.

"Well, let's invite him to have dinner with us."

"I did invite him," he said, smiling.

"You two are made for each other," said Don Ramón as he entered the room.

Europe had recently come out of an outrageous war. Everything was more expensive, but in the end, it hadn't found permanent solutions. The First World War left trauma, an emotional insecurity in everybody. The Western disappointment. The change of values had to be conclusive, and the people would feel it.

On a cold morning, Don Ramón left his existence. The funeral was frugal. They buried him in the common cemetery. Father Manuel performed the funeral rites, and Cipriano fell silent from the grief. For the first time in his life, he endured an incomparable suffering.

In the second year of marriage, Amanda was born. Griselda had three miscarriages. With the little girl, they had done a Cesarean section, and the obstetrician suggested that she have no more children. At the university, Cipriano enrolled in the school of architecture. He received his degree in five years. Once it was in his hand, he read it and placed it back in the envelope. He took it home, showed it to his wife, and sat down on the sofa in the living room. They did not celebrate even though Griselda wanted to share the news with their friends. He insisted they not do so. Juan José had gone to the United States after he finished his first year at the university. They never heard anything about him again. La Bruyére often remembers him.

Outside, the sky is dull, and the lamps in the streets are ready to be lighted in a dying afternoon. Meanwhile, a strong wind attacks with a fury, and lightning and thunder snap the firmament. . . . *Woman, if you can talk to God, ask if I have stopped adoring you at any time. And, love, mirror of my heart, the times you saw me cry over the treachery of your love.* . . .

With discomfort, Cipriano stands up slowly from the chair and scrubs his eyes, which are wet. He goes to the record player and turns it off.

SIX

We are in a large, cold, old room. A massive walnut table shines, and spread over it are sewing paraphernalia: fabrics from numerous regions, sorted by quality and exquisiteness of texture; needles of various lengths; reels of white thread that haughtily offend the colored ones, which are kept apart and are in short supply; white ribbons mainly divided by sizes; beads gleaming solitarily in shallow, transparent plastic boxes; scattered gems of unequal thicknesses in small, ceramic iron plates; and several additional articles for the creation of brides' gowns. Sister Edwina enters the workroom for the second time and has a feeling that it will be the cause of a conflict, a conflict that she has not yet identified but that she interprets as evil. It has saddened her. She believes she hears a muffled moan in the distance, but she does not do anything to discover from where it is coming. She already senses that her mind is deluding her.

Could it be the voice of a nun who is suffering, perhaps someone who wants to communicate with her to warn her of future mistakes, or could it be, even worse, a spirit who wants to test her and make her offend the most sacred of her commitments as Christ's wife?

Without enthusiasm or a greeting, Sister Águeda, an older nun, shows her where to sit by pointing to a bench that is hard, and as she monitors, her aquiline nose causes her to resemble a falcon in search of prey. She tersely explains to her what to do. There is no waste of words, and no assistance is proffered. The smiles have vanished in the group. One would say that everything has been programmed from an immemorial period. Other postulants arrive and sit down around the table and start the construction in silence.

Sister Edwina does not dare look at anyone. The oversized table upsets her. Her nervousness is growing, and she is afraid that it will attract attention. Nevertheless, she cannot determine what is causing her anxiety. She remembers when she was first there and almost couldn't breathe, when the air became thick and a panicky, dry cough escaped. Outside the room, the stillness then renewed and the spiritual peace was restored.

On this second occasion, she has better control even though her discomfort doesn't leave her. She extends her long, thin finger to reach a piece of white silk fabric that would be part of the dress's corset. Her focus is on the movement of her hands. She wants to back up, but she pushes herself to continue. The encounter of the cloth with her index finger hastens her breathing. She does not understand what is going on, and she does not want anybody to notice her struggle that is beginning. She feels a peculiar guilt about something. It doesn't matter what it is, but her rebellious attitude bothers her. She takes a quick break, and she stretches out her left arm and boldly touches the soft, sensual fabric. Pale by nature, she acquires a blush that competes with the redness of her slightly parted lips. The lower one is fleshy and wet. Her thick, black eyelashes opening and closing adopt the role of an obedient fan for her snub nose. She blinks, and an inconsequential smile appears. She tries to meditate about what she has to do. *My God, help me concentrate so that I do not waste my time with banality.* Recapturing her original quietude, she applies what Sister Águeda taught her. The fabric joins again under the stubborn heat of her hands, and she attempts to deny the delight that the connection produces.

The fight will be constant and strenuous. Will she lose?

Sister Edwina is working diligently, as are the rest of the postulants. However, she is far away, in a world with no dimensions and with inaccessible vastness. She has memorized all the instructions, and it is not difficult for her to follow them. Infrequently, the novices share a glance, and there is a collective awareness of solidarity. Each one of them complies without questioning and performs with perfection and always without social involvement. This does not happen when, by accident, Sister Edwina and Sister Leticia Maria look at each other across the

29

length of the table. Both seem to smile even though they are not. There is a kind of unspoken concern, an unguarded empathy, perhaps because during their first days at the convent, they united for the necessity of companionship and bolstered each other's courage. Afterward, the rules of the cloister separated them *because all friendship between the nuns delays the unity with the Lord.* At this instance, neither of them averts her eyes, and both, after smiling, return to their jobs. Neither reveals the least sign of change or amends what was promised.

The bride is very beautiful, like you.

Sister Edwina shakes her head and scares away the possible Evil that takes advantage of her frailty as a woman. The supervisor, distracted by the activity in progress, hasn't detected anything unusual, but the Mother Superior, who arrived minutes before to see how they are doing, immediately registers the curious gesture but doesn't say anything. Maybe because she is familiar with the situation, she doesn't respond to it. Who is not exempt from temptations?

Sister Edwina, her hands often sweeping over the silk fabric, unhurriedly cuts it.

The size is the same as yours.

There is no further disturbance, and nobody notices. The Mother Superior has left the room. With that, Sister Edwina has achieved the creation of a domain for herself. Nobody will occupy the space, it is only hers, and that implies that she exercises her own discretion and disobeys one of the most sacred statements for the perfection of her condition as a nun. She seemingly has no apprehension about her new circumstance, and her conscience does not torment her about her faults. She is serene. She continues tacking at a steady and rhythmic pace, as do the others. Sister Águeda walks, inspecting, correcting, and approving. She proceeds to her own area, where her rosary is, and prays with an absorption that nobody around her discerns. She falls into ecstasies. Her expression changes into one of more contentment. The novices are about to break their silence, but no one speaks. It is the time to finish, and the Mother Superior is in the same state. They gather the unused materials and lay them in their respective containers, and the bell announces that one more chore has ended and that another will begin.

Sister Águeda, having been restored, regains her lead, and orders them to follow her. A delicate drizzle moistens the atmosphere. A little removed from them, the Mother Superior arranges a vase with red roses and sets it at the foot of the granite Virgin Mary in the grotto. She begs for the peace and the salvation of humankind. When they are together again, all of them bow without saying a word, and the Mother Superior speaks with kindness. As Sister Edwina passes, the pupils talk with one another about thousands of worlds, and the older one admits that there are expanses and bonds so subtle that neither time nor doubt can reach them. Sister Edwina realizes a sudden tranquility from being recognized by this woman. It is not that she is being honored and distinguished above her colleagues, but it is in the nature of a surreptitious regard for each other. The novice feels a rapport with the Mother Superior when she is nearby even though there isn't any overt form of attachment or dialogue. Yet all of that is only written conjecture in a great book of improbabilities and mysteries.

SEVEN

The cold weather hardens, and the gray sky blurs a shy sun, which recognizes its defeat against the inevitable permutations of time, In the La Concordia Convent, Sister Maria Esther emphasizes the effort the postulants will need to have in order to obey the bell. *It is God's voice that teaches us to observe the necessary change for our community and improvement of our lives.* She stipulates that from now on, they will have to search their consciences with more care and autonomy, that they should go to the chapel to examine themselves to attest that they are growing close to what the holy rules expect from them. She says that they should be watchful over the minor things: Do not leave the lights on, avoid tardiness, be silent and in communication with the Almighty, avoid the use of words by all means, do not daydream, be humble. . . . In the background, the In Paradisum Angelus is being played by Sister Celeste del Manto Divino, an eighty-year-old nun who has lived in the convent since her admittance, when she was eighteen years old, having never left. The postulants stand up. The weight of the task can be seen in their faces, and it becomes more pronounced with the difficulty that is almost upon them.

"Holy Mary."

"Conceived without sin."

They sit down again. Sister Maria Esther tells them that to profess, they have to rid themselves entirely of the life they had: the family they left, the material things that could bring back the past to their memory, and, finally, to eliminate any reminiscence of their former selves. Amanda, with consternation, slips her hand into her pocket and clenches the rosary that she will have to relinquish even though she does not see a reason to do so. *God, forgive me for questioning. I will give it freely. Forgive me, Lord.*

In the chapel with other nuns, novices, and postulants, she silently prays the rosary. The one she holds is made from roses and has a sentimental attachment. The scent it leaves as she passes each bead over her white and thin fingers elicits recollections of her parents, her house, and the splendid plans she had to become a cloistered sister. The rosary was given to her by her mother in an intimate conversation they had when she was fifteen years old. Amanda asks Jesus Christ and the Virgin Mary to help her become a creditable and useful nun. Above all, she wants to advance in the convent, to be the best, not to stand out above the rest, but to attain perfection and to arrive at heaven. Inside, she cries for this culmination not to be noticed in order to stay away from any condemning self-pride and to never tempt the evil claw of envy and jealousy from any sister.

This afternoon, the veil will be changed. The parents and other relatives and friends could watch from the right-hand section of the church's chapel. An iron door that couldn't be opened was at the front of the room. It was secluded by an amaranthine tulle curtain that allowed a view of an altar in the back. On each side was a high step, and lines of double pews with tall wooden backs of baroque style were joined to the walls. Narrower and squatter pews faced the same direction and left just enough space for the nuns who would be seated behind them. The keyboard emitted Gregorian hymns and Marian compositions. Sister Celeste del Manto Divino spoke with sincerity, and in some way it soothed the emotions, the fears, and any doubts that had infiltrated with the shy invitation to the new call. The candles burned brilliantly, and the flowers evoked an aura of harmony and unique beauty.

Cipriano and Griselda placed themselves on the left side of the bars opposite the curtain. Their hands gripped the cold metal, and their heartbeats slowed and released the battle within them. It will be useless to assume a winner. There are things in life that are better left alone, and this was one of them. The young women, dressed in white with orange blossom garlands and long veils, made their concluding walk as postulants. They were resigning from the past, in which their parents were a marvelous part of their existence, and they also were shutting the last door to the exterior world.

In the appropriate regalia for the ceremony, the bishop, a short man, stood upright. The creamy white miter was decorated with aged rhinestones, and the chapel light reflected the profuse glamour of the chasuble's embellishment of gold, silver, and terracotta threads. His crosier, the sign of his rank, bent with authority and constraint. Standing where the Mother Superior usually did, he reviewed the approaching candidates, and despite his formality, he could not mask his esteem for them. Perhaps, deep within, he remembered that cold day, like today, full of expectancy and exhilarating hopes, when he entered the secluded seminary. His office underlined the influence of a legendary church and the dignity his figure should allude to. He accomplished it. At the center of the church, the future nuns knelt before the lofty Christ and His representative that, united, were giving them spiritual welcome. Nobody smiled, except maybe the Solitary, from His height and His divinity. They were dismissed from the chapel.

Inside, in the sacristy, they took off the white clothing and dressed in the black habits. Their heads were bare, and one by one, they permitted their hair to be cut by crude and large scissors. More than one saw this as a loss of femininity that extinguished itself on the shapeless glass of a decrepit, inexpensive table. The Reverend Mother gave them the upper parts of the habits. The wimples were tied behind their backs and covered their heads and necks and the sides of their faces, and then the tunics were slipped on. Placidly, she looked at the religious women, and her eyes sparkled with affection as the face of each one was engraved in her mind. Her heart filled with love toward them.

The newly ordained novices paraded once more to the chapel and took a position in front of the bishop, who now wore a light lace, over which lay a fine linen amice. He, proud of the small group of beings who were in charge of praying for humankind, asked a straightforward question already known by the novices, "Why are you here?"

34

"Because we want to serve our Lord Jesus Christ, to pray for the world, and to search for the salvation of our souls," they replied in unison.

"If it is like that, and you are not obligated, I welcome you, and give you all my love and understanding."

Subsequently, the bishop received an envelope from the Mother Superior, who returned to her chair, far from him and next to the wall.

"Azucena Abascal. From now on, you will be Sister Mariana de la Inmaculada."

"Praise be to God."

"Luz Maria Hahn. From now on, you will be Sister Teresa del Santísimo Sacramento."

"Praise be to God."

"Amanda La Bruyére. From now on, you are Sister Edwina Marie."

"Praise be to God."

Only silence ensued.

EIGHT

Everything happens at a moment that one doesn't expect. In a simpler way, for example, one sighs, not knowing why we do it, the act is finished, and one is sad because it comes from the soul. Are there moments that totally belong to us? I want to think there are, but I fear that a complete freedom is never ours.

Amanda feels like I do right now. She collects wildflowers, and she divides them into two equal groups. From time to time, she smiles, but the smile is a loner, lacking recipients or complications. She runs down the hill, and a soft breeze from one side salutes her with a hat of sighs. She has to ascend, as the way home is ahead. She carries the two bouquets in her hands, and, breathless, she climbs the path with vitality. She stops and assesses the scope of her twelve years: Beyond that are only mystery, infinity, and beauty.

"For you, Mother."

"Thank you, sweetie. They are beautiful. Are the other ones for the Virgin Mary?"

"Yes."

Thank you, my God, for giving me a daughter like this one. But remember You gave her to me. I don't want to lose her.

In the evening, in her bedroom, when the half moon is seeping through a thick fog and is not able to circulate its charm, Amanda, in her nightgown and on her knees, whispers her night prayers. The flowers are unfolding in a tinplate vase on top of her dresser near a sculpture of the Virgin Mary and a crucifix. At the back of the dresser, the image of the Holy Face, reserved, protects her. She lies down on her bed, closes her eyes, and sleeps. . . .

The hideout is cold. The moonlight spreads silver syrup. The trees wave portents. Amanda jumpily walks on an oval path. The hideout explodes, and the child is left in hostile weather. The Lord's face still watches, but the eyes are bruised and its presence expands. From the forehead packed with thorns streams dark blood. She manages to move her lips, and her gaze is compassionate and, at the same time, judgmental. She stops. Her knees collapse to the rough and wet floor. She opens her arms, and dozens of flowers flow out of her hands, and the perfume pacifies the air from its furious whirls. They confront each other, Creator and creature. The encounter is silent. The emotions are mixed. The interaction is enigmatic, but they understand each other. The Shroud blazes, and an army of seconds repositions an infertile terrain of slowed behavior. Amanda feels that her height shrinks with each passing minute, and she envisions that she will stop being corporeal soon. She anticipates that she will become nothing but will still exist. . . .

"Father, help me. My God. . . Mother, Mother, . . ."

"Child, what happened?"

"Cipriano, she had another one of those dreams."

Griselda forces Amanda to lean on her. Griselda's eyes are ablaze with fright, and she cannot comprehend anything around her. Amanda is her daughter, her only concern, and nothing or no one could change the tie. She needs her, and as her mother, she will guard her from any danger. Time is interrupted, and the terror dissolves into a stream of sobs. Cipriano hurries to the opposite side of the bed. His hair has been unkempt since yesterday, and he has not shaved. His pajama pants and shirt are worn, his arms are bare, and his left arm is in a sling purely for convenience. He scrutinizes her with uneasiness, and his solicitude is unsurpassable. Their daughter is bent forward onto her mother's lap. He perspires profusely. His fingers massage Amanda's moistened forehead. He lifts her brown curls to relieve the paleness of his child's face. He stays composed, and his steadfast countenance reflects all the love he is capable of offering. The storm has passed. Her parents accommodate her needs and then return to their bed. In the dim room, Amanda relaxes, but she is one with deceitful boundaries. The Shroud waits in stillness in the loneliness and quietness of the night.

The next day, before the beginning of classes, the girls play They are in the last year of middle school. Away from the other students, Amanda and Maite are chatting.

"Amanda, I want to marry Pablo, but he doesn't even see me. I have sent him a message, and he hasn't answered. He is a fool, but, you see, I love him. You haven't told me whom you love!"

"I love everybody."

"But Pablo, you wouldn't love him, right?"

"No, he is yours."

"I didn't know that we could love everybody. Girl, you are heading down a bad path. My mother told me that you can love only once, and that you should marry that man."

"Well, no, I love everybody."

The school bell rang. The girls stopped talking and joined the line their classmates were forming. The first break had ended under a heavy sky. All of them were in their respective courses, under the instruction of their teachers. This day, at nine o'clock in the morning, they were notified that they would meet Father Blas, who was newly assigned to the parish. An extra strike of the bell would order them into the main hall. (Amanda, when she heard it, felt a sort of premonition, and stood still, and her sight was lost in an indefinable emptiness.) There would be a presentation of the priest, who came from abroad. Maite knew that he was an exceedingly good-looking man. Her mother had told her how handsome he was, although he had accrued some years. For sure, the forties for an adolescent are old ages. People said he was a man with wide shoulders and a slender waist. He had dark brown hair, a large forehead, eyes of almond color and intense seriousness, a straight and ample nose, and a broad and generous mouth. He also had muscular hands. They weren't exaggerating; I testify that it was like that. But perhaps most intriguing about him was his curly and shaggy beard. He was not the typical priest. He could better be described as a movie star.

The students filled the auditorium. On the stage were a table and two chairs, and the velvet, wine-colored curtains were fastened to the side walls with cords with antique gold tassels, which accented the sobriety and elegance of the room. Miss Benavides Dumont, the teacher of music appreciation, started to play the school anthem, and everybody stood up and remained standing until the end. The principal, Mrs. Beatriz Monroe de Larrea, entered in the company of the guest of honor and asked all to be seated.

"I introduce to you Father Blas Pacelli, the new parish priest and your spiritual director," she stated with graciousness and then went to her seat. Outside, the erratic, blue air pitched.

"Girls, it is a true pleasure to address you. Your principal has reported to me that all of you come from good Catholic families This brings me a singular happiness that you won't be able to understand, but take my word for it. I want you to think that I am, besides the parish priest, a friend who already loves you and is ready to give anything for you. You can trust me, and I am prepared to serve you. The proof that these are not words alone that I give you is that I will now conclude my presentation and declare a day off for you to enjoy."

With that, commotion arose as they simultaneously abandoned their seats in a rush in front of the leaders. The most alarmed one was Mrs. Monroe de Larrea, who had challenged Father Blas and was telling him that it was not practical to do something like this. She informed him that to have a free day, it would be preferable to ask the permission of the Main Director of Education. Furthermore, she advised him, the responsibility would be that of the establishment if anything happened to any of the girls. She was growing more flustered and persistent. Father Blas, unperturbed, scanned the recently vacated room. He slid his left hand across his forehead, touched his hair, which swept his neck and shoulders, and told her that he would pray for San Judas Tadeo, patron of the impossible, that nothing detrimental would occur. In addition, he said he thought that he was doing a superb job and his initiative was already beneficial. He told her that he saw God's love in the faces of the girls, along with their happiness, and he felt optimistic

39

about a positive beginning with them. Still unruffled, he passed his right arm around the principal's shoulders, winked his eye, and left the building.

NINE

After lunch, all the religious congregate at the chapel that burns with light during the afternoon prayers. The flare from the candles sheds colors simulating an orchestra of goblins in the middle of a shattered reality because the world, this world, is a ripple of ups and downs, of oblivion and equidistant hopes of opaque illusions. Each one of them concentrates on aspiring to internal perfection. To reach heaven, it is necessary to sacrifice and to seek humility, love, and generosity in all their acts.

When they return to their activities, Sister Edwina bastes the taffeta with Scottish silk thread, and the sections and gems form an exquisite piece. Sister Águeda leaves her supervisory position, lifts the dress, and approves all the seams. Her acquiescence is instantaneous. She releases a diminutive smile, which rolls to Sister Edwina, who doesn't stop staring at the dress as though it is hers.

It is yours, and yours it will be.

The eyes of a bottomless green do not blink, and the fear in them is gone. They travel as vagrants all the spans of unrealistic, impossible, and remote dreams that one assiduously fulfills with one more act as a nun, knowing that it carries an obligation carded by the years of service. It could be the moment to recall her life outside the convent, but she does not allow herself to do

40

so. She looks at her hands and understands that to be a nun is not a sad way to live but that it is something substantial and personal.

At five o'clock in the afternoon, when the skies wander around and a carriage of clouds race on an unauthentic track, the professed ones convene again in the chapel to publicly confess their sins. They have to walk through the main nave and pass one by one to the presbytery, where each will lie face down, cross her arms, and rest her forehead on them to symbolize a Saint Anthony's cross.

"Lord Jesus Christ, forgive me, I took an extra piece of bread, when there are people who cannot serve themselves with one."

"Lord Jesus Christ, forgive me for being vain."

Silence.

The moment arrives in which Sister Edwina has to confess. It is as though the air has stopped vibrating and wants to hear, with intent, the culpability of a young woman, which will be something to talk about in the convent that works hard in the perfection and the sacrifice. There are no options for individualism and wills without endorsements, or, worse, frivolous vanities.

"Lord Jesus Christ, forgive me for being an imperfect nun."

Silence.

The prioress is attentive to all regrets, and within a minute, is upset. Her gaze is somewhere else, far and cold. She has almost the identical expression as Sister Edwina had when she was looking at the bride's dress. The Mother Superior, however, has a harsher way of observing them. The years make us considerably more cynical.

In revealing her flaws, Sister Edwina feels that the declared fault is an indistinct grimace of a truth she conceives. The temptation is like a pebble that cuts her in two. One suffers because it not only changes the purpose of her mission in the convent but also because it erodes the senses and fabricates a dominion altogether hers, when the individual should not exist; it creates a barrier between herself and the holy rule. She knows it diminishes the process of improvement, and she maintains it in secrecy. There lies her fault even though it is what is in her that has transformed her into a subject of struggle and inadequacy.

At supper, Sister Edwina will recite a passage from the Bible. The dining hall is capacious, and the center is free of any furniture. Along the walls are two lateral tables that are affixed to the walls, with twelve seats at each side. At the midpoint of the room, another gigantic crucifix by an unnamed artist watches over the nuns and notes what is inside them. To its right is the lectern, where the sacred book rests, and she reads aloud as her sisters, with moderation, serve themselves with food.

She finishes the reading. She eats alone.

Do you believe what you just read? Until when will you be deceived? You are beautiful, and nobody appreciates this. All of them want to make you a disgraceful being. The dress and the veil are your size, already perfect, desirable.

She ignores it, and she tries not to be upset, displaying no reaction as she continues. Inside, a racket of worries and fears hammers her fragile body. Each portion of food is an assault on her temptation, and every spoonful is a shout to the silence.

The bell rings from immediately beyond the door. The sound is a pliers on the reality. It is the announcement that if we enjoy an internal peace, everything becomes abundantly clear. If we have a ditch of doubts, the world closes and tunnels absorb us. The oil lamps are switched off, and the darkness envelops the walls with mourning that hiccups with loneliness. The nuns head straight to their cells.

At midnight, Sister Edwina cannot sleep. She turns on the bed. She is in a vulnerable state. The uncertainties whip her. She questions her vocation. She has a need to be loved. She is confident that she was born for better things. She is a servant of God. Her mission is to help mankind with her prayers, her sacrifice, her patience, her humility. Her life, which is not hers anymore and which does not depend on her wishes, should be subject to obedience. She has lost, for love and for devotion, all of her own decisions. She is a being that comes and goes.

My beauty, do not entrap yourself in white lies, fallacious fantasies. You are beautiful.

She, with despair, blesses herself with horror. Yes, with horror. She prays. She starts to faint. A fast sleep wins.

"My darling, how beautiful you are in this dress!"

"Do you really like it?"

"I like it very much. You look precious, my love."

"Are you sure you like it? I feel so insecure, and I am so unhappy."

"Yes, I like *your dress*, but what happened that you are so pale?"

"Why are you in the cassock?"

"What happened to you, my life? Come!"

"Leave me alone! Do not touch me! Let me go! Let me go, Father! Let me go, Father Blas!"

The night no longer restricts her. She leaves her bed, she places her hands together, and the index fingers touch her shy lips. She is motionless for an instant, shivering from the cold, which also is inside, and everything becomes more complex, more disturbing. Rushing, she resumes the prayers, prayers she learned when she was a little girl.

I am sure that you are more beautiful than the bride, the dress is yours, only yours, yours.

She opens and closes her eyes in desperation and confusion, and she blesses herself again and again. She is calm, but it is a frosty calm.

. . . Lord, don't test me anymore, I beg you, come to my aid, help me. I am weak. . . .

TEN

In the distance, the pasture has a turquoise hue. The country house is stately. It was built more than one hundred and fifty years ago, and it maintains its majestic beauty. The façade is imposing with its composition of white walls, moldings, and columns; the substantial, carved, dark walnut door; and the profusion of windows with thick glass. In the back, a terrace surfaced with an Italian tile and trimmed with flowerpots is circled by a balustrade, which allows a view of a horizon of mist and idle dreams. The owners once had their breakfasts on the terrace during every summertime, with their four terriers and two Afghans, but for the last few years, the family has not made use of this tradition of previous generations. The miniature gardens at the entrance remind one of the grandiose palace grounds of elegant France and Claude Monet's paintings. The stables are my favorite part of the estate because of the Anglo-Arabians and a Boulonnais, Champion, which belongs to Lord Milton and which is the only one he would ride. All the horses eat from large stone bowls, swinging their tails.

Their daughter, Elizabeth, has red hair and light green eyes. Her face is pleasing, but her grace, her characteristic since childhood, calls the most attention to her. When I met her, she was sixteen years old. I admit that more than once, the abundance of her hair bothered me, and I had the terrible temptation to tell her to cut it. On other occasions, I experienced a velvety sensation

44

that I couldn't understand and that, at the same time, gave me chills. But who was I to suggest something like that to a woman? (I was an adolescent and an apprentice of love.) I was quiet.

Lady Ashley, her mother, was ill and spent the majority of her days and nights in bed, bored and with around-the-clock nurses. The white color was predominant in the curtains that accumulated implacable discussions about mortality. With the deficiency of concrete information, a web of stories had been woven about her. People talked about a refined but unapproachable woman. Others would say that she was a despot. They even said that the marriage just worked in appearances and she was not well because of a failed suicide attempt caused by some slip. She never recovered.

Lord Milton, an austere gentleman, did not socialize much because of his wife's illness. He shut himself off most of the time in his library, paneled with ebony wood and fitted with furniture of the same material, all of which gave an impression of a certain beleaguered darkness, saved by the generous lighting, thankfully, and by the ample windows. He was tall and lean with a heavy beard and deep-set, blue-green eyes. At home, he wore a cashmere robe in the cold seasons and a short, cotton robe in the warm ones. He was the owner of an extraordinary quantity of books, especially focused on philosophy, history, literature, and theology, and he was an ardent Catholic and friends with the pope and some missionaries from Africa and America. His relationship with the bishop from his city was tepid but cordial. Whenever I saw him, it was from a distance, and to me, he appeared to be a gloomy and introspective man, maybe unsociable. I admired his sophistication in all his acts. Lord Milton would arrive in the fall, meticulous in a striking MacFarlane and a hat that matched. The chauffeur, an insignificant being, was not pleasant, and his social resentment drove him to a disgraceful behavior. He hated everyone, and I wasn't an exception.

One day, I found Elizabeth and John Bentley kissing, and I was affected as never before. She had fallen passionately in love with him, an American student from Oxford.

"John, you have never kissed me like this."

"Elizabeth, remember that I love you like no one else could ever love you. Every time our lips met tonight, I wanted it like it was the last time."

"John . . ."

The night threatened, once more, with being fateful, impenetrable, and dangerous. The moon, for its part, kept fluctuating in a perpetuity of mysteries and profound soliloquies.

John was affable and talkative, and his personality made all of us appreciate him. He was quite tall, he had light brown hair and plentiful freckles, and he spoke with a drawl. Many remarked that he somewhat resembled the film actor James Stewart. With everything ready for the wedding, the groom did not return. He had disappeared with no trace.

I remember Elizabeth did not leave the house for a lengthy period. After a time, she would ride her horse, Tempest, for hours, in her riding dress, or she would devour a book in the library, but she was always alone and with a far-off gaze. When I wanted her to meet with me, she agreed with my requests but persisted in her obstinate loneliness. I intoxicated myself with my need to see her. I did not try to write to her, for I realized, right away, that what I would say was nonsense, that it, thrown into the wind and into the hidden eye of the moon, was a vague plea to the poetry of the Sevillian Gustavo Adolfo Becquer or to the tormented and impetuous Lord Byron.

As the months went by, Elizabeth became more taciturn. She would go out to the town early in the morning and would come home for supper. Her father did not question her, but only watched her, and he sank into a terrible depression because his two women, as he used to think of them, were gravely ill. He let his walks by the gardens and fields become less frequent, as were his outings with Champion. I recall that it would fascinate me to watch him ride, sometimes in a languid trot and, at others, hurling through the crumbly and humid fields of some morning that would spurn its damp night for a young and innocent sun. The reading of his most cherished books was more habitual. An apathy and a disillusionment of life would settle on his face, and he recurrently fell asleep in the rocking chair, where he read. When he would wake up, he would be upset because he hadn't had enough rest or the opportunity to analyze and deliberate. He would eat sparingly.

One day, not sure if it was a dream, the aridity of his thoughts or the cloudiness of his existence was mixing everything in a shared space empty of separations or of realities. His face painted the distress that would afflict him. He fell ill. The bishop came to visit him and sat next to his bed the whole morning. He departed, meditative. He mulled over the confession, which was completed through rasping breaths, that he had listened to over the past hours. He became tearful because he realized that, inadvertently, he had not sought his friendship. He acknowledged his oversight, and, too, that he would not have accepted him as a friend. With measured steps, he walked away, he entered the diocese's automobile, and the chauffer drove him from the Miltons' property.

Elizabeth more and more was acquiring a restrained and pensive aspect that I did not like. It wasn't fun anymore to be with her. My interests shifted to other things, and she lingered as a suppressed remembrance that one day had excited me, although I should state that it had been the first time that I had had fantasies and also the first big disillusionment.

Elizabeth seemed to have found an indisputable peace. She looked after her father with devotion, and her work was similar to a religious who was familiar with the essential tasks for curing bodies in hospitals full of beds and medical crews. Lord Milton was suffering from an acute melancholy that prevented him from functioning with normality. Elizabeth was in total charge of her father's condition, but he never recuperated. She alternated her activities between her parents. The nurse was still with her mother, but the daughter controlled everything that concerned treatments. Her father passed away.

Her sadness was stronger than her endurance, and for an afternoon, she was distraught. Regaining her senses because of the duties that she had assumed, she continued her final endeavor. She dismissed the night nurse, and she took over the care of her mother. She attended to her and occupied and dedicated herself to prayer for two years. Her mother also expired. In black, at the cemetery, she received the condolences, and she thought that she was hearing the same ones she had heard when her father died. She did not accept the offer from anyone to accompany her when she left the burial ground. She drove her dark green Ford back to her home to confront the shadows. She discharged the personnel who worked at the house. She called a taxi. She looked one last time at everything. She made sure all was in order. She closed the main door. She had with her the plain clothes she wore, a purse, a white envelope, and her black overcoat. She abandoned the place, giving it a silent goodbye, and never returned. She was twenty years old. I had set sail to a faraway sea for a while.

"Elizabeth Milton. From now on, you are Sister Maria Esther del Niño Jesús."

"Blessed and praise be to God."

ELEVEN

"I was waiting for you to come out of the church," Sister Edwina said. Having seen Sister Maria Esther in prayer, she had stationed herself at the door to talk with her. "Now I know whom I should emulate."

"My daughter, I thank you for the generous and benevolent compliment. But you couldn't be more wrong," corrected Sister Maria Esther, who stopped at once and retained her characteristic smile. It was there, but the borders were subtle and impassive. "One should emulate only Jesus, our Redeemer. With Him, nobody can be wrong. We humans are miserable beings that are always looking for our own advantage. We do not provide for the needs of our fellow man. We do not have charity, and neither do we have the longing for the good of all. If we examine our hearts with objectivity, we would find that what is within them, warning us, is egoism and the I, I, I that takes over our behavior entirely." She said this with circumspection and humility, and the emphasis apparently fell on some personal, dusty tale of constant repetition, perhaps years of conviction, of presentation, of making it a habit. The private is relegated to oneself and never should be revealed. Maybe it would thereby be converted into a force, into a reason for being.

"I have been trying to find you since the other day because I wanted to talk with you. When I saw you communicating with our Lord, I was sure that I had to ask you for advice. I am overwhelmed and worried, and I am not happy."

"I can do so little for you in this case. It would be better for you to talk with the Reverend Mother or with Father Blas. They are the experts. I am no more than a nun."

"Nevertheless, I looked for you. I know I can talk to you without weighing what I can say or not. Afterward, I won't feel bad, nor will I regret doing it."

49

"The mirrors of the soul are cavernous, whose crevices have ceased to have form. Silence and solitude are our authorized weapons of survival. I cannot recommend enough prayer. Pray always, become accustomed to conversing with the Lord, and search for Him. Let the rosary make marks on the palms of your hands so that your heart will overflow with relief and peace."

Sister Maria Esther would not avoid an appeal but would only permit a minimal amount of interaction between herself and others. The rule should be to comply without errors, without excuses. It started to sprinkle, and the nuns headed to the convent. Persisting in the air was a vapor of silence braided in ambiguity and unfinished dialogues.

Sister Edwina was pacing in her cell as she steadily regarded the floor and squeezed the bulky rosary hanging from her belt on her right side. She then began to inspect the barren walls. The coldness of them and their gray existence would lead one to think of irrational isolation whose purpose was to enhance holiness by means of self-deprivation, the continual negation of any instinct or human feeling. One should suffer to benefit from it. One has to love the Nazarene to find salvation. Soon, she veered toward the narrow, uncomfortable bed, this sort of shroud of vulnerable contradictions to any normal possibility. The crucifix above the headboard had coagulated blood on some parts in an intensely corporeal sheen. She knelt down with an internal lament. It was a mixture of sublimation and hopelessness. She was quiet and obedient on the outside, but inside, her crouching rebelliousness was rising. She couldn't share with anyone her despondency. That it could only be discussed with the Lord or the Reverend Mother and, in some circumstances, with Sister Maria Esther, began to upset her. She entertained the idea of looking for a manner of communication with other participants in the immense-small place where she had chosen to live of her own will, but she couldn't attempt this because the rules of the convent prohibited it. "The rule, the rule, the . . . rule."

Her parents came to visit her She wanted to touch them and hug them, but the sentiment would revive in her a reality that was not in shreds. The expression on her face was of unbounded bitterness. Also, Maite was coming to comfort her, bringing her gardenias from her garden. Maite knew Sister Edwina was a person devoid of meanness, destined to be a perfect nun, but she lived outside, and Sister Edwina, the anomalous, inside. Sister Edwina sensed that her space was the worst of the entire congested world where the evil spirit dominates and all in his entourage were happier than she was. Then she—the martyr, the intruder, the foolish, the different—was suffering and was being asphyxiated by the deceived. Today, accompanying Maite was Adrian, the one with the guitar, the one who was carrying a bouquet of white roses with one single red one in the middle. Far away, with a lot of concentration, one could distinguish a slight, plastered smile of the guilt, present guilt and the need to be succinct because moments in life are *strikes . . . so strong . . . I don't know! // strikes like God's hatred, as in front of them, // the dregs of everything suffered // would take over the soul. . . . I don't know!* We are very much tied to those verses, we have clung to those verses that so many times translate our anemic state of mind! She made the sign of the cross because God does not hate anybody, not even evil ones. Adrian had given her the roses, and the perfume and verses confused her, and although she was sure to tell him "no" when he asked her to date him, his kindliness, her gratefulness for him to have noticed her, and his company alone were still whipping her sometimes, and "once in a while" could be a euphemism to say "always."

In her discouragement, she remembered some lines: *Your judgment, Lord, terrifies me like it is thunder. Shocks of fear tremble all my bones, and my soul fills with terror. I am astonished, and I consider not even the heavens should be pure in your presence. If you found evilness in the angels and did not forgive them, what would become of me?* She raised her eyes, and she thought of herself as a grain of dust facing the Creation. Also, she visualized the acorn the pigs eat. . . .

Troc, troc. Troc, troc, troc. A nun walked the corridors that divided the cells, announcing it was time to rest. The lights were no longer on, and she removed her habit. In bed, she prayed the rosary, allowing it to leave its impression on her fingers. The numbness put her to sleep.

Without causing a sound, Sister Gertrudis entered Sister Edwina's cell. She watched her as she slept with her hands entangled in the rough rosary. She examined this face that showed remnants of a terrible ordeal oscillating between fatigue and resignation. She extended her hand, which trembled from her emotion and guilt, and skimmed the line of Sister Edwina's hair. She smiled with illimitable peace. She resumed her initial position and called, "Sister Edwina, Sister Edwina, wake up."

"Yes. . . . Oh . . ., are you Sister Gertrudis? Is something wrong with you?"

"No. Or yes. I want to talk to you."

"You know that we cannot do that. We already broke the vow of silence."

"I am the one to blame. I have to tell you something. Does it bother you to listen to me even if we break the vow?"

"Of course, if it would help you, I am with you, but we have to write it down in our books of personal evaluation and ask for forgiveness publicly."

"I decided to leave the convent." Her disclosure had a power that even she didn't recognize.

"But why? You seem to be doing well. I had thought so in my prayers. Happily. I healthily envied your vitality." She was disoriented.

"My life is a hell. I do not believe in anything, and I need companionship. I made the wrong decision."

"Are you sure?"

"Yes. I am convinced, Amanda."

A silence gravitated amidst the doubt, the candor, and their fate. Sister Gertrudis observed her sister with affection and admiration. Sister Edwina, fixed in the stare of her visitor, was trying to penetrate the dark almond tulle of Sister Gertrudis's eyes but was having difficulty comprehending what had happened. Her predicament was cut short. Sister Gertrudis went to the bed and sat down on the edge where the sore hand was shielded beneath the blanket. Sister Edwina backed herself to the wall so that Sister Gertrudis would have more room. They were mired in the opacity of the cell. She became nervous about the episode that was escalating, but the repentance in both of them was not important right then.

"I am just saying goodbye to you, Amanda. I know that you will be an extraordinary nun and you will be dedicated enough for both of us. Forgive me for my selfishness, but I had to talk to you."

"I am happy that you did. God will better interpret this farewell that for me is so hard to accept. I will miss you, Asunción."

The eyes of both of them filled with tears, and on an impulse, Sister Gertrudis hugged Sister Edwina and whispered in her ear, "I will always carry your smile with me."

She did not say anything. She couldn't. After the pause, they stayed like that for a while. Sister Gertrudis quickly kissed Sister Edwina's forehead and left her. She did not look back. Sister Edwina kept her eyes closed, and a heartrending cry made her grab the blanket and cover her mouth to smother all her anguish. She leapt off the bed, seized her habit, and rashly charged off to the chapel.

Lord, I need your help in this moment of confusion. You have to come to my aid in this quiet torment, unworthy of a wife of yours. I don't know what I want, what I truly need. I cannot even present myself or give you proof of my restlessness, of my sense of oppression, of my uneasiness. You know my soul. You know what is happening to me. Help me, Lord. Take this chalice of death away from me. Give me peace and comfort in this gap of my formation. Help me because I am overwhelmed, and I am not content.

Sister Edwina would hold up her hands and would connect them just to separate them afterward. She would leave her knees, and she would stand up. Once more, she would lift her hand to her mouth. Her eyes, saturated with tears from grief, wanted to communicate all the more her irresolute state. Recklessly, she stood up before the great crucifix. She raised her arms and embraced herself to Him. She left, not considering that her fingertips might have mistakenly encountered that which gives life. It is life that one fears, one loves, and many times, one can't understand. She wouldn't rebel, she wouldn't dare to offend, but she needed a minimum contact, a physical joining with this mere magnum of affirmations and absolution.

Why do you not follow Asunción? She is not a fool. She doesn't want to be a useless nun. She is not weak. She knows what she wants and is determined. You are more beautiful, and you place yourself in this world without life, with no prospects. If you leave here, you will have peace. You will live with normality. Men will desire you. You will be the most enviable bride. You will fulfill your woman's role. You will be a mother, . . . be a mother, . . . be a mother. . . .

Sister Edwina noticed that the air was feeling heavy. Seconds later, the severe pallor in her face subsided. How much time had passed? The minutes are skirting boards of destiny whose seeds disguise themselves in nothingness.

TWELVE

"Amanda, it is time to wake up. You hurry up, beautiful."

"I am coming down right away."

"Father Blas, if the girl has any flaw, it is that she is very lonely in her room. She has her own world. I should confess that Cipriano and I worry a little about that. She goes to school alone and returns the same way. Her only friend is Maite. When she comes here, they stay in her bedroom, and no one hears them."

"Well, Madam Griselda, I don't believe it is anything serious. Retrospection can only indicate a lot of internal composure that we could wish that everyone had. Besides, you have told me that she doesn't give you or Cipriano any trouble. I am glad that she is a sensible girl and quiet rather than one who would cause you problems. I very much like that she is kind and that she prays with discipline. She will be an exemplary wife and mother. Or, who knows, perhaps turn out to be an excellent nun."

"Don't say that, Father Blas, not even as a joke. She is my only child. Recently, I have been hoping for many grandchildren. You see, God wanted me to have a daughter only. I had three miscarriages, and with the last, I almost died. I am alive because Saint Jude Thaddaeus interceded to God for me."

"Good morning, Mother and Father Blas."

"Amanda, your father left for the fields early, but Father Blas is having breakfast with us."

"Good morning, Amanda. You are looking very pretty, as always." Father Blas went to her and studied her and passed his rough hands through her light hair. He held his hand over her

55

head and soon lowered it to her left cheek, letting it rest on her tiny jaw. She, until then, had been looking at him and smiling faintly, but feeling the prolonged pressure on her face, she glanced down and closed her lips.

Father Blas, along with a solid posture and energetic actions, had a strong voice, which could easily arouse the insecurities and concerns of the parishioners. His demeanor was casual and friendly. The rural life and the missions in the jungle were part of all the obligations that he had to carry out in a range of locations. Now, he found himself in the parish of the town of La Bruyére. He did not ask how long he would stay or whether the new appointment would be permanent. He settled into the pastor's residence. He did not have many material belongings. There were three trunks of books, some theological-philosophical essays and drafts, and some manuscripts of sacred and secular poems. He arranged the books on inexpensive shelves and hired a middle-aged maid.

The life close to nature, in a perpetual struggle with the gusting wind, the never-ending drizzles, the unmerciful downpours, and the missionary work with the unassuming populace in the countryside had framed within the friar traits that the other religious did not have. Also, the combination of his informality, his Franciscan beard, and his assertiveness bore no resemblance to any other religious. But despite that, he is a spontaneous character, compassionate, well-intentioned, charitable, and forthright. Father Blas is one of those men who captivates women and relates well to other men.

For breakfast, Griselda had prepared orange juice; bacon; crepes with broccoli, mushrooms, and cheese; blueberries in citric sauce; and sweet rolls to serve with black coffee. Also at the table were fresh fruits. Father Blas thanked God for the food they were about to eat and gave a heartfelt blessing to his hostess. He had one more portion of everything, praising all the food.

Griselda, pleased, cleared the table, and Amanda began to wash the dishes and utensils. He removed his pipe from his pocket and asked permission to smoke. When they consented, he took out tobacco, which he kept in a kind of bag, pressed it into the pipe with his right thumb, and lit it with the match Griselda provided. He savored it as he leaned back in the chair, delicately gripped the pipe bowl, and again expressed his gratitude to God and Griselda.

After remaining like that for a while, he stood up and stepped to the window. He opened and closed his lips as he exhaled the smoke so that it formed circles, and he marked how they melted into the enormity of the remote place. Once, he pulled the pipe from his mouth and inserted the stem through one of the smoke's unfolding rings. Preoccupied with his accomplishment, he smiled at life, life that for a hermit could be noteworthy. His thoughts were being lost in the lengths of the pastures, and time was set aside for another prank, one of many that made his personality strong by the vivacity of his prayers and his mischief. What would the monastic man with green eyes be thinking? About the parents he had abandoned? About a woman who had made him quiver and doubt once more his vocation? About the sacrifice his Savior had made at the cross as proof of the ultimate love? About a passionate kiss that he never gave and never received? About life? About how we are born to die and perhaps die to live?

A gathering cold allowed itself to intrude upon the atmosphere. It was coming from behind the mountains at a tortuous gallop. The religious became anxious. He tapped out his pipe, and the tobacco's residue fell where the grass was growing next to the house. Griselda and Amanda had finished, and he went to them, hugged them, and then kissed both on the forehead. The silence was revealing a lot. He smiled, made the sign of the cross, and left. All of them were delighted with the visit. Father Blas walked rapidly through the town's narrow streets. On high, the clouds were threatening, and a moment later, the storm began. Mother and daughter parted, each to do her chores. They thought about the absence of Cipriano and that they would have liked him to have shared the unforgettable breakfast. After all, it was like it would have been recorded in the wind: The essence of things continued in suspense, and everything else happened as something intrinsic in the tasks of that vast space that we know as "once upon a time."

The days paraded by with their routine. The air was growing colder, and the gusts frayed the leaves until they fell and lay motionless against the damp, autumn soil.

"Mother, I would like to go to Maite's house. She has come three times to visit me. Can I go there now?"

"I know you have finished your chores because, if not, you would have asked me in another way."

"Yes, Mother, I have finished."

"Then you can. Don't be late, and I would like you to be here when your father comes, to welcome him with me."

"I will be. Thank you, Mother."

Amanda crossed the room to where Griselda stood. She held her close for almost a minute and gave her a kiss on the forehead. She sensed that something was different, something she hadn't been expecting, and it was banging at the doors of change in their lives. There wasn't anything written or safe ahead of them. There was only an indistinct feeling that was producing sadness and fear.

THIRTEEN

Sister Edwina suddenly leaves her bed and clasps her hands together. Her index fingers touch her lips. The cell shifts into a breath of wariness and bewilderment. She hears faint noises that lead to nothing. She reacts with apprehension and wants to escape. She realizes her limitations, and she remembers her promises and is frightened of her lies.

She is still for a while. Shivering, she prays, racing through the prayers she has known since childhood. That they do not soothe her does not make sense. Yesterday, the Hail Mary was motivating, and today, in this moment, it is like a cold waterfall, fast and superfluous. Her eyes, wide open, question the incertitude and the dread encasing her soul, her invisible core of self. A pinkish perversion entices the evil in her. Her white nightdress of a rough fabric is tight-fitting to her body that shudders with foreboding, turmoil, and anticipation. What happened? What are you afraid of?

I am sure that you are more beautiful than the bride. The dress is yours, only yours, yours.

Tremulous, she closes her eyes and opens them wide again. She briskly makes the sign of the cross. The gown dissolves on her, floats. There is a thought that will seduce her.

Something deep within her shouts, moves, charges impulsively, unconnectedly. She once more catches the nightgown. Her hair sways with the unrestrained motion of her head, and her right hand tries to tame it. Her eyes, her eyes are out of control. There is no celestial support; there is no angel to defend her. The rosary has lost its spiritual inspiration. The solitude envelops her. Far away can be heard an unusual, indecipherable echo. She directs her right ear to an imprecise point. With her left hand, she holds the nightgown, and with her right, grips the part that folds across the chest and tugs it over herself. Everything is in vain. It is necessary that she should go to the chapel, to the Virgin Mary's altar. It is her one assurance. She has no other option. She harbors a hazy confidence.

She dresses in the habit. Without permission and with quick steps, she leaves the cell. She is perspiring, and the darkness surrounds her. The door is closed. She pushes. She hurries to the lateral altar of the statue of the Virgin, Our Lady of the Smile. She kneels on the first purple prayer stool. She crosses herself. She raises her eyes, which are moist and grieving. She enters into communication with her. One does not know what they say because the tone is low, imploring. She begs for quietude. A long time passes.

The Superior pulls her veil gently. At her touch, she is not afraid. Notice of a close and peaceful, familiar being will calm her. She smiles. They exchange an inseparable dialogue with their eyes. She stands up. The Superior takes her by the shoulders, and not touching her face, pretends to kiss her on each of her cheeks. She crooks her right index finger and points at the door. Sister Edwina has a few seconds to say goodbye to the Virgin. Again, she glances at the Superior, who studies her. When she leaves, the altar has a minuscule luster, and of the Superior, there is just a shadow.

In her cell, already on her hard bed, she is asleep. A vast prairie extends in a valley wrapped in grass and tiny flowers. She is barefoot, and her feet welcome the freshness of a sunny morning. Pastoral music plays in the breeze. Fauns with miniature, cinnamon-colored flutes dance to their music, which is defined for her at the end. She appraises herself in a giant mirror. She is a shepherdess who drags a covered basket. The docile sheep trail after their leader. Now and then, she touches one with a cane, and the animal jumps and changes direction. The others change direction, too. The basket is heavy. She arrives at a hill, and a chime resounds in the valley. She bends and peers at all sides, and there is no one. She conquers the summit and descends to the other valley, where the waters of a sapphire river doze undisturbed and sprout into the silences. The sheep drink. She does the same. When she is wetting the palm of her hand, she sees the god of the forest behind her. It is a male goat with medium-sized horns, with the face and arms of a man, and with a profuse beard. It plays the flute with ardor. The eyes reveal that it is possessed with a clumsy passion. The body and the feet are of an animal. By instinct, she hastily grabs the basket, but it opens and her habit flies. The faun watches her with fatal rage. It moves its lips and utters its thoughts.

You are beautiful, Amanda. Better than the bride. The dress is yours. It is ours.

She swiftly stands up from the bed once more and untangles her gown. She makes the sign of the cross again, and she quickly prays. She invokes all the saints, the Virgin Mary, and God Himself. Nobody answers. However, a short, censorious laugh comes from close by. It is a mockery, a wind that burns certainties.

Minutes later, the troc-troc of the brass that a nun carries awakens the others. Sister Edwina is already dressed, ready for a new day. In the church, the religious take their respective positions. Father Blas energetically starts the Mass, reminding them that with this act, they recall the sacrifice and death of the Divine Redeemer. The faces of the religious at dawn resemble sleepwalkers at a leaden twilight. Here, with the limited gleaming of the candles, they revive the vigil, and the sad Christ doesn't seem so alone.

"Hail Mary."

"Conceived without sin."

It is the moment of the consecration, and the priest, in the higher altar, turns and faces the community. When making the sign of the cross with the host held between his index fingers and thumbs, the eyes of Father Blas and Sister Edwina meet in a personal, oblique point at the cross that is formed. The attachment is fragile, negligible, but it is witnessed in the dreadful theater of the improbabilities, with the faun's hint in the middle of the crystalline, pastoral waters. She looks down. Her hands bend, and her lips unite with her skin softened by the pain and ambivalence. One Lord's Prayer, three Hail Marys, and one Glory to God briefly seal the failure of this novice. After the last prayers of the group and then the blessing of the officiating priest, the congregation prays with a remarkable devotion and meditation. Sister Edwina also finds serenity. She breathes with an evenness that alleviates her nervousness.

After a meager breakfast, she is assigned to her chores in the garden. Immediately, she goes to the rose bed. Her favorites are the white ones with splashes of crimson. She pulls out the weeds and thinks she is one of them. She sorts the rocks that were scattered around yesterday by the storm. When she is done, she rakes the dry leaves into a pile and picks them up along with the ones that are about to fall from the bushes. The thorns threaten. She is pricked and bleeds. Reflexively, she lifts the finger toward her mouth, but she stops. She prefers to let the blood drop on the perfumed whiteness of one of the petals. The color is precise. For the first time, she feels that she has contributed something to the universe. It is a healthy satisfaction in the middle of the risks of life.

Nuns and novices meet at the church for the middle morning prayers as the nun at the altar sings the *Beata Dei*. The religious reassemble in a group like a black bouquet for their meditation. Any problems they could have, in this instant, would be odd and insubstantial. Looking closely at their faces, none of them shows discord, and all of them are tranquil in their silence, accompanied by the shimmering of the candles and the Gregorian chant.

After lunch, Sister Edwina and the other novices will care for the birds, sweep the chicken coop, clear up the hen run, and collect the eggs from the nests. She likes Sussy, the cream and red one, which comes running when it sees her because it knows that her benefactor has something special for her, generally a piece of bread. She loves to hear her boooock, bock. She would say it is her best chore, although she is fond of all the animals in the enclosure: the geese, the ducks, and the partridges. If her workmates weren't there, she already would be talking with her barnyard friends, a breach that couldn't be reported.

After they clean, they will round up the Jersey cattle and drive them into the barn for milking. The milk will be for the *dulce de leche* that the sisters of the kitchen prepare for the assortment of candies and the popular confections they sell to the public. Most wanted during the year are the meringue fillings from their homemade marmalade, the Saint Claire's sweet bread, peanut butter eggs, and those containing *Pío V*. They are proficient also in harvesting royal jelly. Their beehives are well tended, and the technique has been with them since the opening of the convent. Besides the selections of hors d'oeuvres, completing the repertoire of delicacies for every occasion are salt and sweet breads, quiches, and desserts.

At the chapel, they pray aloud. All day, they have not spoken. The rosary, as well as repeating the Son of God, the Father, and the Stations of the Cross, is monotonous but is reassuring because it unites them and strengthens them for any impending uncertainty. They live in an eternal present of adoring their Lord and asking for forgiveness for their sins and for the entire world. They leave the chapel and go to supper. The reader starts, and the others, who have been eating, listen to God's Word. They finish and retreat to the vast library, where they read any book that is available to them. Sister Edwina is engrossed in the volumes about the lives of the saints. Now, she is about to finish the biography of San Juan de la Cruz.

In her bedroom, she prays once again, she meditates on the sacrifice of the generous Jesus, and she embraces the rosary and closes her eyes.

FOURTEEN

"Sit down, Sister."

Silence is the acknowledgement.

"Well, what do you want to talk about?"

Silence answers.

"Do you have no words? Is it something very serious? You are pale. Are you feeling well?"

"I am well. Better said, I am well physically, but I am in trouble because I don't know what to do."

"I hear you."

"How do I tell you?"

"From the beginning." Her voice is sweet and mollifying. There is a delicate smile on her face. Her eyes seemingly hold a presentiment. The sister is not clear that it is there, but she can sense it.

"I don't want you to take this as a complaint because it is not. But I cannot keep on like this. It has been days since I have been able to pray. Worse, neither can I concentrate on my work."

The tears are authentic; they are not a dramatic feminine quality with little importance. The novice is truly distressed. Suffering.

"Reverend Mother, I have exhaustively examined myself, but I haven't gone to Father Blas yet. I believe that I should talk with you first so that you can tell me what I have to do. Sister Edwina does not like me, and I can't accept her attitude. I want to thank God for this test that He puts in my path to make me better. But I can't take it anymore. I feel weak. I am weak. Her indifference and her demonstrations of superiority hurt me. Sometimes, I wash the garden and stables and scour the tools when it is not my turn, when she is the one who should do it. I intervene only to offer to God my hurt for her inexplicable conduct. When I finish, she thanks me."

"You should talk with each other," she interrupts.

"We do not speak. I was about to say that she thanks me with a condescending air that makes me feel empty. I run to the chapel to ask forgiveness because I have begun to hate her and also to ask God to change my feelings. I don't want to be in this situation anymore."

The Superior withdraws her gaze from the sister's. She places her hands together as though she is about to clap. She holds them close. The eyes have fled to other worlds. The minutes die away. The silences pause. With short steps, she heads to the window. There, the air passes unvaryingly, and the clouds, on a wedding trip, throw orange blossoms wrapped in murmurs of pearls. She meditates. She assembles memories. She fears. Her head moves up and down. Once again, in front of the novice, who is leaning forward with expectation, she urges her to continue. Searching the pupils of her supplicant, she cannot quit thinking of the green eyes of Sister Edwina.

"I don't understand why she behaves like this with me. But I noticed from the first day that she didn't like me. While we were reaching for our veils to dress, I took hers by mistake, and right then, I apologized. Amanda did nothing to forgive me. She joined the postulant who was leaving, and with her, yes, she was all smiles and politeness. On another occasion, there was a last piece of bread on the plate. It was mine because I was there first. We were next to each other in the same line, and I took it. But seeing her disappointment, I handed it to her. She did not so much as attempt to show me any appreciation. She took it, and she walked far away from me. I am like a leper in her life."

There is a gap in time. As one sobs and fashions imaginings of a better life outside the convent, with bustle, laughs, drinks, succulent dinners, and pleasures, the other, the older, wanders to the vague remembrances of her youth and her first intimate friends. But everything has been so far behind that even the perfume of those recollections has no presence and lies broken in a corner of the mind. However, an incident like this, which comes with no summons, introducing itself through someone's crisis, opens its own wounds that remain for a while and remove themselves without leaving scars.

"My daughter, I recommend that you be cautious when dealing with Sister Edwina. Do not seek her out. When you meet with her, think that she is your best friend. Pray a lot for her. Love her. Accept this cross that will unite you with our Savior, the one who gave His life for all of us. Pray for you, for me, for the world, and do it now more than ever. Let's not permit evil to enter our hearts or our house. Let's banish him out of our lives, and let's learn to be the true wives of Jesus Christ. Do not doubt His love and mercy. Entrust yourself to Him in every circumstance. Let's offer Him all our beings, and let's accept sacrifice as our present. Let's not expect awards or sympathy. Let's give all and request nothing. He will take it upon Himself to help us, and let's offer sufficient thanks for our salvation. This is our final goal."

I come for you to help me and not for you to come up with the monologue that I have heard so many times, thinks the novice.

"You have changed suddenly. What happened? Are you not well?" The Superior has begun to be suspicious. By ritual, she picks up the crucifix that is resting on her right leg, and she rubs it with her fingertips as she starts a dear prayer.

"No, it is nothing. It would be—" She hesitates and then adds impertinently, "But if Sister Edwina had been here instead of me, how would you have treated her? Would you have had the same opinion? Would you have given the same advice?" Her voice has lowered. Her eyes have acquired a red tint around them. The novice is palpably annoyed, and she is becoming more upset even though she wishes to maintain the composure of a true religious.

"I cannot suppose anything, but if Sister Edwina had called at my door, I would have received her in the same way that I have with you, my daughter. Why do you have the idea that it would be different when you know it would not be?"

Apparently more sure of herself but trying not to look at the nun, the novice leaves the chair and shoves it backward. Blind to the landscape beyond the window beside them, her thoughts roam. She dries the cold sweat from her forehead, and she blows her nose gracelessly. She wipes away the white saliva that appears on the edges of her lips, pivots, and says in a threatening tone, "Call Sister Edwina. I want to ask her while looking at her eyes what she thinks about the bride's dress that we are sewing for her. Call her, I tell you."

The Mother Superior abruptly stands up. She tries to confront the eyes of her inquisitor. The novice avoids them. She doesn't want her miserable views to be impugned by this woman who does not understand her and does not advocate for her. She realizes that the Superior probably is aware of her own preference, and it is for her enemy.

In the meantime, Sister Edwina has left the chapel. She is at peace. She has volunteered to clean the chicken coops again. She wants to be entertained by Sussy's chicks that have just been born. Yesterday, she checked her nest, and of the twelve eggs that were there, three had opened. The chicks already were chirping around the abandoned eggshells and were thrusting out their tongues to the wind, which was fluttering across them. When she saw her the day before, her friend was distrustful and irritated and was pecking because she was defending her young. She did not accept the bread. This time, she takes another piece in case she has changed her behavior.

Drawing near, she knows something is wrong. A sulfur odor is spreading throughout the hen house. The floor is sticky. Across the room from her, swarms of flies are flitting, tumultuous over the abundance of excrement, feathers, and blood. Sister Edwina immediately feels cold. She runs to the nesting area. The rosary is slipping on her fingers. Sussy lies beheaded close to the chicks that are calling franticly for their mother. Her panic forces her to see that the faun has slit the head of the one she favored.

The Superior Mother stops and, noiselessly, holds up the crucifix from her desk. She makes the sign of the cross in the air, and thousands of petals of Forget-Me-Nots drop gracefully, coating the floor in pale blue. The novice, out of her mind, runs away.

Sister Edwina begins to lift up what is left of Sussy. In this second, she feels the stab in her back. She sees the faun coming closer with the tool that just wounded her, and he is doing it again. The rosary falls from her hands, and she wakes up with the troc-troc of the morning.

FIFTEEN

The vows are chastity, obedience, and poverty. The postulants, the novices, and the nuns of any convent need to abide by these fundamental rules all their lives. There are no interludes and no exceptions. The advice given to each one of the candidates is that she should prevent the first fall so that there would not be a second.

Sister Edwina is in the chapel meditating. She is sitting in a pew with her eyes closed, and fitfully, she rolls the rosary over her hands. Every Hail Mary is a chain of illusions added to her desire for mortification in order to conform to the perseverance of her sweet Lord. In this interval, her thoughts uncontrollably take her to the moment of receiving her novice's habit. There, they dress in white. Their veils, held by crowns of nards, cover them from their heads to their toes. They parade, feeling that they have arrived at the place they have been seeking for years. It is the accomplishment of all their hopes. They are exultant, and in their inner joy, neither the sound of the keyboard nor the smell of the incense can distract them from this sublime event. They are closer to fulfilling their dreams since The Call captivated them. In minutes, they will realize all their aspirations. None of them wants to reconsider. All of them have decided, with incredible sacrifice, to obey and to dedicate their lives to prayer, to the labor of the convent community, and to the wellbeing of all.

The two rows of younger postulants, wearing their brides' dresses, walk forward to receive their habits. On the elongated walnut table, adorned by a pearl-colored tablecloth washed with indigo bleach, are the items that will belong to the future novices. The Mother Superior bestows a benign smile on them, but it is lukewarm, impersonal. With solemnity and a lost gaze, almost absently, she gives a black habit, a wimple, and a veil to every one of them. There is no physical contact. It is an obligatory relationship, but perhaps the description is not exact for the track left by each one of the postulants. The treatment is not perceived as odd. They have become accustomed to it in the six months of training, practice, and imitating the aloof conduct, somehow icy but innate, formal, and indulgent. I cannot stop commenting about the appearance of the Superior. She is lonely, without ties, without preferences, tall, slim, famished, languid, and with a far-minded look. She is incapable of inviting confidences or initiating a simple salutation. She is unsocial in the middle of a mystical world, whose goal is to supervise her sisters in the convent in instructing the postulants in dedication and purity.

The sacred music flows throughout the spacious room. The nuns as one group analyze their future sisters in their slow walk, these novices who will assist them in the illustrious, pious effort that needs to be done and who will eventually occupy their stations. Sister Edwina recalls the six months that have passed since her father left her at the convent. It has been a time during which she accepted the discipline and the adherence to the rules and, moreover, disposed of any question or doubt about her ability to take her vows as a sister. It is not that she is not sure of her vocation, but she sees that the path to perfection, the detachment from any self-serving act, and the denial of any intimate, anticipatory, and corroborative reactions are problems that cannot be explained to the Mother Superior or Father Blas in order for them to counsel her. She feels that she is an imperfect religious about to surrender.

Another worrying aspect is to accept unconditionally all that will lie ahead. The search for the humility to fully devote herself to her mission is something that she would like to relinquish, for it is so hard to harm oneself consciously that any person doing so would become gloomy and develop an exhausted disposition. The exercise has to be daily. One should enjoy deprivation to achieve spiritual glory. Nothing will have merit if zealous obedience is omitted. The silence in the case of Sister Edwina is easy because of her temperament. In some ways, she is a loner, and the requirement naturally befits her personality. The most ardent give up spontaneity and do what they are told in the way they are told to do it. Almost every day, she writes in her book of internal examination: *I accuse myself of not obeying once more the holy rule. I allow my instinct to take over the situation, and I do not meditate on it or on how my God wants me to do His wish.*

If it were a temporary thing, unnoticed and involuntary, she would endure the torment of guilt every day. Until now, to come to the church and to be alone and with no excess of light, restores her and comforts her to the point that she has a tenuous optimism that she will attain peace and know that she is doing what her Lord wants. But just by leaving the refuge, remorse consumes her.

For six months, Sister Edwina has lived as a postulant. Today, she won't be one anymore, and she will start her novitiate. Until now, she has been taught the spiritual life and the daily routine of a nun. Henceforth, she has to reassess whether The Call is real and whether she is destined for a holy and sacred existence. The nuns, for their part, have to judge her sincerity, character, and ability to coexist in the community.

During the ceremony, each postulant is sponsored by a spiritual mother. Sister Maria Esther is the one who has educated and guided Sister Edwina's candidacy with care. Also, she sewed the white bridal dress that has to be used on the day of transition. The design is austere, unembellished. She wanted the veil to have her individual touch, and so she attached two delicate silk appliqués to it and embroidered it as she used to do with any other garment. The minute detail was impressed upon it because she is feeling like a mother who is giving away her daughter, her only daughter, in marriage. In some ways, as a woman, she would find fulfillment, as if her child is entering a life that she could guarantee to be the best and most complete.

For Sister Maria Esther, something else has to be done. It is a reluctant task, but it is compulsory. In previous investitures, some of the postulants shed tears during the hair cutting because it was the last drop of femininity that remained in them. It would float freely and with reservation and would circle the cheeks that have lost all color, like faded white lilies. Cautiously, she releases the hair. She lifts it at the right side, and as the scissors are clipping, emitting a mean sound, they both chance upon each other's eyes, where they stay focused throughout the process. Sister Edwina detects that her mentor is having an uncomfortable moment and smiles at her with sweetness, an encouragement to carry on without guilt. Sister

71

Maria Esther recognizes the approval, and her face lights up. Finally, it is a not-so-short hairstyle in order that the wimple and veil would be suitable as a symbol of the candidate relinquishing the vanities of the world, of the demon, and of the body. From now on, she will use the habit of her order, exclusive of the white veil that still identifies her as a novice.

It is also the ceremony during which they renounce their names and adopt another in honor of the Virgin Mary or any saint of their preference. The bishop who presides over the ceremony presents a lighted candle to the novice while announcing, "Amanda La Bruyére, from today on, your religious name will be Sister Edwina Marie." When she first thought about the idea of becoming a nun, Amanda wondered why she needed a new name. Later, she understood its relevance. Sister Maria Esther explained to her that the transformation is biblical, as, for examples, when Abram was changed to Abraham, Jacob to Israel, Simon to Peter, and Saul to Paul. All were renamed when they gave their lives entirely to the service of God.

During the period of the novitiate, the candidates study the rules and the constitution of the community in depth. They become immersed in the practice of mental prayer and adapt themselves to the mortification, the absolute negation of their self-interests, and the teaching of the Holy Church. No secular readings are permitted during this time, but they learn the Gregorian chants and the history of the Church and of their order of nuns. The novices, in general, never leave the convent except at Christmas, Easter, Corpus Christi, and in an emergency involving close relatives, to visit with them.

My Lord and God, forgive the actions and excesses about which I address you. I thank you for your goodness and compassion, for your daily forgiveness, and for your eternal love.

The light of the chapel is turned on, and the shadows are playing hide and seek and spinning mysteries by the dozens, evaporating and leaving a trace of suspense.

SIXTEEN

It is two and twenty-six in the morning. Sister Edwina does not sleep quietly. She is perturbed by the naked light bulb on the ceiling, which hangs hushed and lifeless, wrapped in the muted reflection from the hallway. She believes that set in the core of the bulb is a labyrinth that forges a game of tag between her and a wizard. Who would want to complicate the life of a nun, her life? She sees flying staircases that invite her to climb up, but a mink stole and silk fabrics encumber her hands so that she cannot securely hold on to the handrails of one of the shorter staircases chosen by chance. She slips frequently and drifts in the air, clothed in her nightgown, but the air prevents it from totally covering her. There is a fight for preservation and modesty and, far away, a secret yearning for freedom.

Hovering, the wizard of the bulb is each minute maneuvering closer to her, his facial appearance reconfiguring itself into a distorted similarity to the seditious and sluggardly faun, who, with his traditional flute, whirls to the rhythm of a deceitful and sensual music. Soon can be seen a hill with sequins in the middle of a valley with a foggy grey pasture in some sections, and bright in others, and whose vegetation rocks in a presumed breeze that does not rest, but hurls. Cutting the air are thousands of scissors, and parading in disorder are hundreds of pins whose tips pierce the sleeping bodies that want to be far from the walnut table and the tin receptacles. The flowers, the majority of them white, also careen with equal intensity.

I have to specify that even though the nun is burdened, riddled with unjustified remorse, she is innocent. In this volatile setting in which she finds herself, she wants to hang on to something.

73

The rosary cross that she grasps in her left hand enlarges for moments until it reaches excessive dimensions but is reduced in an instant to a pitiful insignificance because this time, it cannot be the lighthouse that illuminates the anchor that holds and stabilizes her. The forces of lust are in charge, and the defense of any mortal against them is a frail passenger in the imaginary pathways, which she perceives between the night and the cell, between the dream and the wakefulness. I was hearing her moaning through the thin walls that separated her dwelling from the other rooms, but I did not recognize any of the language.

Afterward, there is a short interval in which the nun relaxes and allows her fingers to wander over the rosary. It is a recess of celestial peace; it is a knot of hopes in the middle of a chasm of misgivings, of sorrows and bad beginnings. *You have to refuse all calls from the body. All bodily instincts nest in concealed pleasure and threaten the life of the community and the salvation of the soul.* The nun changes her posture, the rosary falls to the floor, and, inadvertently, her eyes are detained by the lighthouse, which is brightened by a light filtering from the corridor where the religious sleep. Nothing but starkness is in the convent.

She is awake. Cognizant of what she is about to do, she rises, dresses in the habit, and puts her shoes on. Without a sound, she leaves the cell. She tiptoes to the sewing room. There is a breeze that invigorates her. Her walk is both majestic and mundane. Her short hair acquires a certain shape, as though it is being combed by a long hand and slender fingers. One can appreciate her walk. She is a trim, self-confident woman, and the furtive rhythm of her hips achieves more and more agility and independence. The habit is unnecessary. Nothing intimates that she is out of breath or that her anemic state can experience a twinge of contrition. No, now her need is different.

74

The bride's dress is almost finished. It is draped with a rustic material, hiding the delicacy of the gown. Twelve nuns manufactured it under the expertise of Sister Águeda, who could replicate every stitch, backstitch, and decoration. Strongly, she tosses back the cover. There is a shameful luster in her eyes. She sees that the right sleeve is basted. Remembers. She smiles with indecency and lifts her arm toward it. She stretches out her hand, and she notices its hesitation before the moment of its first brush with the material. She breathes more rapidly. She suffers a culpability even greater than before. She is at the point of fleeing. What is she doing here? What compels her to commit such an unprecedented act? She should leave immediately and run to the chapel and throw herself on the floor like the most miserable of creatures and ask for clemency from the God who created everything.

Amanda, the dress is yours. It has been done for you. You tailored it. The others were your helpers. You are so beautiful. Try it on.

Go, try it on.

With caution, standing again in the middle of the unlit room, she locates the place where the candles are kept. She takes one. She lights it, and it sheds a feeble glimmer. She breathes with anticipation. She strips off her habit and the nightgown. Naked, her nipples are erect, and she is enclosed by the trousseau of darkness that kisses her ivory white skin. She has the trembling of a woman about to be possessed. The dress fits her perfectly. The right sleeve, unstitched, tumbles to her feet, and a whine of nymphs perforates the air. A pin stabs her, and she bleeds just enough to leave a permanent spot on the silk. She does not realize it. A wolf howls from far away. Sister Edwina wants to ignore what she heard. Brash and resolute, she hastens to the sheet screening the back wall and pulls on it, and a towering mirror, the single mirror that exists in the convent and which is kept veiled, is disclosed. It only has life when a bride tries on her dress and has to walk the runway to rehearse the last details of how she will wear it on the happiest day of her life.

Sister Edwina stands on the pedestal and turns on the lights, and her reflection appears. With her hand, she straightens her reddish-brown hair and assumes a pose of a *Vogue* model. She accepts what she is doing with no regret. With determination, she admires and evaluates herself, and for the first time, thinks that she could possibly have another life, one that has been hindered by a kind of egoistic membrane that has wanted to deprive, to rob, and to deceive the most human instinct: the satisfaction of being a woman. She moans, breathes deeply, and allows herself to feel virginal.

You are beautiful like no other, Amanda, my Amanda.

"Yes, I am beautiful."

"Sister Edwina, what happened? Have you been worried? I am aware that you have been alone. Sometimes, it is not recommended to let yourself be so solitary. All of us love God, but we also have to be conscientious and worry with our brothers and sisters. I discover you in the farthest recess of the convent, here where there are plentiful gullies."

"Father Blas, you surprised me. You are right, I was very far from here. It is curious that you said 'gully.' That is how I feel, in the middle of a precipice."

"Can I help?"

"No, not now, Father Blas, you cannot help me. In reality, nobody can." She is letting the words pour out with no forethought as she looks at the floor, now visible with the light from the sun barely present.

"Is something disturbing you?"

Father Blas is insisting, although he is mindful that his company is not desired in these moments. But he is sensing that this elusive being is carrying a cross, and he can't forsake her, not only because it is his responsibility to save a soul from trouble but also because he likes this woman. He has always liked her, since she was a child, and he has a fondness for her that he does not have for the others.

"I will not suggest that you confess to me right now. But I want to invite you to open your heart and talk to me because I want to be positive you are all right."

Stirred by her dejection, he firmly takes her arm. She answers by leaning her body backward and lifting her eyes from the floor, and they are drawn into his penetrating, green eyes. From a distance, anybody would construe the two religious as a couple about to embrace in a moment of passion under a sky frugal in colors and in the depth of an indiscreet corner of the convent.

The eyes of the friar link with those of the nun. There is no dialogue. The world is still. The roles are about to change. Sister Edwina is in control. She allows herself to be driven by her impulses. Slowly, with tenderness, she moves closer to him. Her left hand, quivering, touches the friar's neck. The other encircles his waist as she stands facing him. She moves even closer to him; she has the same fervor she had the night before in the sewing room. She moistens her lips and after drinking from them, she bites them and presses them into his fleshy ones. She recoils, thrusting him from her and freeing herself, and in despair, sinks her fingernails so fiercely into his athletic arms that they leave depressions. Once more, their eyes join and engage in a struggle between them.

"You cannot do anything for me! Let me go! Don't disgrace yourself! I am not worthy of your respect! Let me go! Let me go, Father Blas, and treat me as vulgar . . ., as a prostitute. Even they are better than I am."

The crying overpowers her, and, exasperated, she runs from the room. Father Blas remains behind, immobile, stunned, with no thoughts, confounded about what to do. He raises his right hand to his chin, touching it many times. He breathes in the suffocating air, pulls out his rosary, and begins to ask for wisdom. The afternoon becomes dark, and the howl of the same wolf echoes from afar.

SEVENTEEN

"Blas, come down. We don't want to be late."

"I'm coming, Papa."

He stops reading the comics and leaves the room. He bounces down the steps two by two, making fists and sliding his knuckles along the railings. He hurries through the door, closes it, and goes directly to where his father is waiting with the car running. It is a sunny spring Sunday, and the parishioners congregated at the church are eager to attend the rite of the Mass. They are in their Sunday attire, the women, in colorful dresses and almost all the men, in black. Within the church, a communal devotion is evident. The sermon by Father Bernabé has well-received results, for all the parishioners are attentive and prove their appreciation at the offering, which the altar boys, in red and white vestments, collect. At the end of the ceremony, the priest stands at the vestibule, and the people say goodbye and bid one another a good day.

"Where are we having breakfast today?"

"I don't care. But I want pancakes, and a full order, okay? I want them with maple syrup and bacon."

"What a sweet tooth! Here we go." Father and son look at each other, their smiles broad, and the car leaves.

In the restaurant, Rogelio Pacelli seats his son and takes the seat beside him. He smooths his son's hair, regarding him with pride, and his fingers become entangled in the copious, light brown curls. After he jiggles his hand loose, the child responds with another smile. He is eight years old and is wearing a coffee-colored coat; short, grey pants; a white shirt with a multicolored tie; knee-length socks; and boots the color of the coat. His grey cap, which he removed when he was at the door, is at his side.

Rogelio reviews the menu. "For my son, an order of pancakes with bacon, maple syrup, and a small glass of orange juice—"

"No, I want half," interrupts Blas.

"A half glass of orange juice." He emphasizes "half," and both of them are amused, but the father is a little more so.

"For me, a half glass of grapefruit juice, black coffee, and eggs with bacon."

"I will bring it right away."

There hasn't been much discussion, and Blas returns to his musings about the last book he read. His ambition presently is to become a sailor. He wants to search for buried treasures, to fight in the rough sea, and to defend, and not to hunt, whales. He is eager to have his own boat, to operate telescopes and compasses, to plot new routes, and to make a fortune. Also, he wants to be an architect like Rogelio and design admirable buildings in his hometown. He would like to be the best after his father. He drinks water while he waits for his breakfast, and through the window, surveys the resplendent stretch of beach by the exceptionally blue ocean.

His father also has his eyes set in the distance. His memory is a valley of images scattered with sighs and mournful nuances. Angelina passed away soon after giving birth.

"Rogelio, you bring up the child well. Look after him and love him for the both of us. God has given me two minutes more to have him in my arms so that I can give him my blessing and say goodbye. I have just given him a kiss, and it is my entire legacy to him."

"Do not try to say anything, my love."

"You make sure he will not commit the mistakes I did, that . . ."

Rogelio's eyes have become wet, and he tries to dry them quickly. He thinks Blas has overlooked his brief somberness. How wrong he is!

"Here it is," says the waiter, arranging each one's dishes. Ingratiatingly, he smiles at them, confident that the smile is friendly and wide in order to receive a generous tip for his hospitality, promptness, and first-rate service.

The silence persists. Rogelio leaves behind a heartbreaking remembrance, but Blas does not. *Why do you suffer, Papa? You got upset because I asked for a half glass of orange juice? That can't be the reason because if you didn't want to give it to me, you would have said so. I know, it is Mama.*

When Blas was six years old, he met Father Joaquin, the director of the seminary and the priest responsible for vocational training. He also was a sublime preacher at the Christian retreats. His oratory was moving, and his tone of voice, strong and convincing. In simpler terms, he conveyed scholarly interpretations of Christ's words.

"Father, my last confession was last week."

"Yes, my son. God hears you."

"I don't have big things to confess—perhaps that I like to sleep a little more than I should, and, sometimes, I don't want to pray the rosary because I prefer to write or to do something else."

"Do you pray by yourself?"

"No, we, my father and I, do every night before going to bed."

"How old are you?"

"Twelve."

"Have you thought about what you would like to be when you grow up and become a righteous man?"

"Yes, I want to be a priest."

"I suspected that. Did you tell your father about your intentions?"

"Yes, I have mentioned it to him. He has explained the good and the bad of being a priest."

"The bad!" He raised his voice and scared the boy.

"Yes, the bad." Regaining his composure and to protect his father, he also was stressing what he was saying.

"How is that?"

"Well, I won't have children and a beautiful wife to love and who will love me."

"What do you know about having children?"

"Well, I know everything. I am twelve!"

Father Joaquin almost let out a hearty laugh because of the firm manner and the spontaneous and defensive way he was saying it. "All right, my son. I want you to be here tomorrow with your father at two o'clock at the convent, and we will talk about this. Is there something else you want to confess?"

"No, Father. I repent my sins and ones I don't remember right now, and also, I promise not to fall into any temptation."

"As penance, pray only one Lord's Prayer, meditating on the beautiful prayer that Jesus Christ taught us in order for us to achieve eternal salvation. God bless you in the name of the Father, the Son, and the Holy Spirit."

"In the name of the Father, the Son, and the Holy Spirit. Thank you, Father Bernabé."

The interview was conducted at the indicated time and place. Blas did not attend the school but enrolled in the San Luis Seminary. He studied with determination. He was an exemplary seminarian, and he learned many languages. Days before his ordination as a priest, his father passed away from a heart attack. When he was about to enter the institution that would prepare him as a missionary, he had a solemn conversation with Rogelio.

"Papa, I thank you for your support and blessing that you have given me for my calling."

"You shouldn't thank me for something that I do with all my love because I am glad that you follow the calling of Our Lord. I will bless you every day of my life."

"Even so, I am sorry for two things. I won't be able to give you grandchildren, and I will leave you alone. If you ask me now not to go, I will not."

"Blas, I could never interfere with what you want to do. I also feel sad that you won't have children, and because of that, you will never realize what you are to me. I am sorry that I won't be able to play with my grandchildren when I am older, but I will be compensated for everything because you will enhance the lives of so many and will lead so many more. You also are carrying out the ministry that I at one time thought about doing. My son, again you have my blessing."

His first job was at a poor parish that couldn't afford a permanent priest. Afterward, he was educated in Rome and then went to Ecuador, to Quito, where he stayed nine years offering spiritual guidance while visiting hospitals, prisons, and hospices. He traveled throughout the Amazon jungle, acquainting himself with primitive groups and relaying the word of God to the provinces on the coast where no priest had entered for many years. He was evangelizing the people of the high plateau. Later, they named him chaplain of Santa Clara's Church. It was there that he met the Bruyére family.

Father Blas spent most of his time alone. He was still writing and reading about philosophy, theology, and fiction. He found solace in the hours he passed praying at the nuns' chapel. He would plead for world peace, for the West to recover what it was losing: the traditional Christian values. He would beseech God for the salvation of the souls. He would commend himself to the Virgin Mary, to Saint Joseph, and to the Child Jesus to be a worthy priest always and to take his apostolic work to the ones who needed it the most. His concern now was Sister Edwina Marie; he wasn't sure what to do with her. He brought his right hand to his chin, stroking it often. He took a deep breath, and with his rosary, asked for instruction. Time was paralyzing, and only some imprecise notations were falling on a light cream-colored paper. The afternoon darkened, and he heard the howl of a wolf once more. He paled and shook himself and left his thoughts by his side. The evening overtook him with a ponderous murkiness. He stopped writing.

EIGHTEEN

It was raining. It was raining as usual, and agitated halos around the streetlamps gave off a faded glow while the insects danced furtively and insecurely from the lack of raincoats to protect them. A stronger light was coming from the chapel, and the choir of nuns was singing a Marian song. The moon, hiding, was listening as it glided between clouds.

Immediately after the afternoon prayer, Sister Edwina went to the backyard, to the boundary of the convent where the gullies nested. A residence was there for the elderly nuns who had completed their decades of labor and who had begun to enjoy even more the proximity to God. They were beautified by the constant prayer, the daily mortification, and the forgiveness of their sins.

With purposeful steps, Sister Edwina entered. She shook herself, flinging droplets of rain from her cape. She wiped off her shoes, opened the arched door that sequestered the constricted foyer, made the sign of the cross, and headed to the right where six older women were individually praying the rosary. Each of them, I am sure, thought God would assist her in dying. There were eight beds with white sheets and quilts, all pristine, and beside each bed was a nightstand that held a plain lamp, a Bible, and a small box for any use. Above every headboard was a cross, the most rudimentary style of all: two coffee-colored sticks of wood tied by a cord of a matching color. At the back of the room was a massive painting of the Immaculate Conception with the most sincere smile an image can portray. Sister Edwina looked at the nuns, but none of them did anything to indicate that she was present. She took out her rosary and prayed as she waited for them to finish.

Startling them, the sky reverberated with the roar of imposing war planes that crossed the air, which, confused, was opening itself from the might of human invention. The rain had stopped. Man and technology were initiating a period that would change people's behavior. The

84

anguish and the isolation of the people would be emphasized. Where is the moon? *Black pony, big moon . . . An icicle of moon . . . Rails of moon . . . dark of green moon . . . should swim in the moons . . . Under the gypsy moon . . .*

The nuns made the sign of the cross because the onset of the end that would descend over all had been announced. Sister Edwina first went to Sister Constanza de la Immaculate. After the consent and smiles for each other, Sister Edwina repositioned her in her narrow, metal bed so that she was more comfortable. It was known that this religious was a close friend of Griselda and had met Amanda when she was a child. For many years, Sister Constanza de la Immaculate was called the nun of the stigmata. She also had the fame of levitating while praying, and around her was a scent of fresh roses. She was short, dark-complexioned and had almond eyes. In her later years, she gained weight, and it was now difficult to ease her aching muscles. After assisting her, she gave the others her regular affection and attention. She took a little more time with Sister Apatia Maria because she could feel the sting of the blisters that were left by the nails hammered into the palms of her hands. Sister Apatia Maria did this to withstand in life the agonies of purgatory or, perhaps, of hell. Her gaze was lachrymose and dull. She never smiled because the Lord had planted in her the seed of a terrible conviction, that upon death, one is forsaken at the abyss of nothing. For more than seventy years, she had endured her torture. When all were settled and had offered every breath and every heartbeat to the Divine Beloved, Sister Edwina switched off the light and turned to them with an expression of goodbye, and the darkness closed over the room.

Outside, in the world that did not exist for them, everything was changing. In 1929, authoritarian regimes were violating or eliminating liberal constitutions of the majority of the poorest countries in Europe. They were fighting because of social reforms, nationality, and religion; they were bearing mounting cuts with every economic crisis and foreign threat. . . . *The world is in chaos, men are suffering, the earth shakes, and the air is assailed with omens. . . .*

Sister Edwina foresaw the events that were about to occur. She arrived at the chapel. Kneeling, she asked for safety, and into her thoughts, she found a minute exit from her quandary. The Lord would shelter them from any future threat, but what would happen now that the Nazis were advancing and would destroy everything in their path? She pushed her hands together and laid them on her forehead and prayed until the early hours of the morning, through a night crammed with presages and troubles. She fell exhausted to the floor, the kneelers inverted, and she stumbled through hundreds of honeysuckles and a creek zigzagging upstream until she was in a village full of lighted cottages and dirty roads where there were no inhabitants. Her solitude was alarming. A long distance from her, she saw a yellowish-white light, and she couldn't understand the state of ecstasy in which she found herself. The light was approaching her with so much vibrancy that she couldn't move, and the fear and the powerlessness abandoned her. A silhouette of an angel was cloaking her and was carrying her through the lustrous blue skies, and her happiness was limitless. Unexpectedly, the benevolent, radiant presence withdrew, and she was flying by herself to a place even more illuminated. She heard a strange call, reassuring and articulate. She raised her right arm, and her index finger made contact with something she discovered and she wouldn't dare to pronounce. . . .

"Sister Edwina, wake up. You have to go to your cell," a tepid voice was saying.

She was opening her eyes slowly. An upset face was becoming distinct above her.

"Why are you interrupting me? Why don't you leave me alone?" she said flatly, diverting the embarrassment of her beginning.

"Come with me, Mother, I will take you to your bed."

Sister Clementina del Manto Divino, the nun on duty who announces the minute to wake up, supports Sister Edwina as she stands up. This time, she is tired. It is the first occasion that she needs assistance. Something is happening to her. She walks slowly. In her cell, she undresses herself. The one who is caring for her notices stains of fresh blood from the waist down. She lifts the modest garment and observes that a fine barbed wire has encrusted the nun's flesh. There aren't cuts or a bad smell. She finds only the sacrifice, as punishment to the body and as hope to reach heaven, that this being has accumulated for years.

A notebook in the immeasurable night is creating caricatures of moon, of wind, and of mist. The imaginary town bellman is reviewing the clamor and the whispers of the creators of an apprentice in struggle.

In the distance can be seen the silhouette of a friar walking in the semidarkness.

NINETEEN

"Sister Maria Esther, I have to talk to you. Thank you for receiving me."

"It is my duty, Sister Edwina. It pleases me that you have made an appointment with me."

"Since I have finished my novitiate and because you are my spiritual mother, I want your opinion about my behavior and activities in our institution. Do you believe that I am ready to take my vows?"

"Yes, my daughter, you are ready for your temporary ones. Remember that you have three to five years before receiving the permanent vows. Have you thought about what to study at the university?"

"Yes, Mother. I want to pursue careers in philosophy and theology, if they allow me to do both. If not, I will choose one of the two."

"You had commented once, during our conversations, that you were interested in becoming a university professor. Why is that? Is it because it has new possibilities in our order for other, less traditional activities, more related to the service of the people?"

"I believe that is it. When I was very young, my father told me that he was the first in his family to hold a university degree. It impressed me, but I had no idea of exactly what he had accomplished. My mother explained it to me, and afterward, my parents, together, told me that I was going to be the first woman in our family to graduate from college. I have always kept that dream. On occasions, I told Father Blas about it and that I wanted to renounce my request for the mortification, and he assured me that it wasn't because of vanity or conceit. When he realized that it wasn't that, he forbade me to carry out my sacrifice."

"I agree. You have my support. But clarify this for me: How will it benefit our order? What type of apostolic endeavor can your university diplomas offer us?"

"I like teaching, and I do not care where I will teach. Also, I want to write about philosophy and theology. I love it. In between the required readings in the convent, I read the biographies of the saints. I was captivated by Sister Juana Inés de la Cruz, and I decided that I would like to follow her example because I want to be a nun who will be an asset to our community."

"Good, I am satisfied with your judgment. I will make the pertinent arrangements for you to attend the Gregorian. We will lose you for some years, if that would be the choice of the Almighty. You would be the first nun from our order to receive a doctoral degree in both disciplines. I will recommend that you earn both. God bless you, my daughter."

"Thank you, Mother."

"Do not forget that the vows of the religious orders are so that the candidates can imitate Christ in poverty, in chastity, and in obedience. Also, so they can comply with His invitation: Go and sell everything you have and follow me. Nothing is yours. You do not have anything. You do not own anything. You have to share everything with the religous of your community. You only need the essentials to live and to subsist. If you need something, you will have to ask permission. You cannot buy anything without authorization. You cannot receive any presents without the approval of the Superior."

A brocade of clouds speeds up its gears in the heights of the infinite. A sharp light reappears in the crest of the sky, and translucent rays are arrayed implacably over the dome of shadows.

"You will have to remain a virgin always, always; always. . . . The purity will be kept by any means. There won't be any excuses. All of these will be given by the love of God for the rest of your life."

Naked bodies appear in a gigantic canvas. Adam and Eve look at an apple, and the flavor of the fruit could be tasted, and the alarming nakedness is sheltered amongst thorns and roses.

"You will have to willfully forfeit your needs to those of the Superior. You won't be able to enter or exit the convent without authorization. Your former aspirations cease to exist when you are a nun of the community."

Everything is in a complete mess, the walls and chains and fire. Authorities' index fingers point, calculating the site of travel the spot of the inevitable. Pincers with cutting edges rush in unannounced. Distances, memories, decisions are in bewilderment, only threatened by conflicting desires. There, there is the anchor, the boat has hopes.

"These three vows signify a total surrender to the Almighty as the model of life. Every professed religious will be given a crucifix to be hung around the neck to lie against the chest, as well as the silver ring, symbolizing the marriage to the Lord, that will be worn on the finger."

Finally, Jesus will be mine, and I will be His. What else could I wish for? The entire world couldn't satisfy my heart because it belongs to Him, whom the angels adore. I unite myself with my God, my beloved King of the heaven and the earth, and I want to remain as His wife forever.

Therefore, I, Sister Edwina Marie, promise to follow, to never abandon the vows of poverty, chastity, and obedience, our Divine Lord and the Blessed Virgin Mary. To the angels and saints, the entire celestial court, to my superiors and successors, in accordance with our sacred rule and constitutions, I hope by the grace of God to persevere faithfully until my death.

Amen.

The nun is slowly treading back and forth in her cell. Her right hand grabs the beads of the rosary suspended from her waist belt. With anxious rhythm, her left hand shields and pats the crucifix on her chest. Thoughts crowded with uneasiness, sweet concerns, and false visions prowl. There are her footprints on the rough wooden planks, abrasions that testify to the tortuous life of Sister Edwina. She paces, staring at the floor, refusing any advantage of a respite that sleep grants. In due course, the nun who awakens them will come, and she without sleep is prompted by a dilemma of decades. *Lord, make me an instrument of your peace. Don't remove my suffering but permit me to do your will, which is also mine.*

Kneeling on the floor, searching for the most offensive grooves, she prays.

She does not have intentions to wonder about whether she could have another way of life. A different one is not for her. What she cannot set aside are those memories of when she lived with her parents, of her school, of Maite, and of her dreams that were shared with no one. She lays her head on her arm. Sleep wins her over. She closes her eyes and visualizes a sea with emerald waters and a boat, with a canopy of biting steam in the form of a cassock, that sways. The clouds play with her subconscious, and then an enormous paper with a giant pencil appears that writes something about her on the white, ethereal base. Afterward, mum figures in movement, gawping, some with lost and soulless eyes and vacant faces, are anticipating, in spite of her appearance, her tragic, eternal destiny. And in an obscure distance are the blue eyes of the young man who used to watch her secretly, and she could not discover why he was interested. He was good, kind, dressed in sadness, and desperately lonely. They only talked a couple of times, together under a maple tree whose leaves shone tarnished gold in the fall months. The years are wounded when we want them to be our havens.

Troc, troc, troc.

TWENTY

Father Blas can't sleep. A moon, his moon, his only moon, marvelous and far away, passes through his large, rigid window on a race of omens, determinations, and predictions. He strolls with a stoop and with his eyes looking down and his face on tenterhooks. It could be said that his thought is a burst of oppressions and worries galloping at the rhythm of inquisitors' steps in a cramped, narrow cell bereft of any comfort. *What tortures this being who comes and goes but waits and loves?*

At the corner of the bedroom, the attendance of the moonlight provides a glimpse of a portable Remington typewriter with a blank page in it. Dispersed around it are a range of writings, loose Marian poems, reread novels, several essays, philosophical and theological researches, piety booklets, a catechism, a worn-out Kempis, missals, dictionaries, saints' cards, and rosaries. Nothing is heeded. The gaze, when it tilts upward to the sky seeking changes, is unreadable, loaded with mysteries, sorrows, and shadows. Nevertheless, at the bottom, perhaps concealed, is an alliance of contradictory rejoicings for this face that cries out for mercy. He knows what has to be done, what should be established, what has to be forgotten, and what has to be expressed.

Troc, troc. The morning nun with her customary tread wakes up the religious. Each of them bounds from her bed, makes the sign of the cross, places her hands together, and touches her lips with sleepy index fingers, closing her eyes full of religiosity. The nightdresses cling tightly to the women who do not value voluptuous shapes. But the smothered emotions remember that although the body is despised, the body is the center of what is being disguised and denied.

At the chapel, the nuns pray, sing, meditate, regret their errors, and make promises to improve. A timorous breeze weaves through the burning candles and the sacred images. The religious are tranquil, except one.

Back in her cell, Sister Edwina, brooding, packs her belongings bit by bit. She was not able to sleep, and so she went alone to the chapel in the early dawn because praying sustains her when she is distressed. Her confusion is besetting her. She is a religious on the border of despondency. She is feeling that time and space are constructing her discontent for a yesterday and a today that are the present. What she fears is the future that will be the present and unmercifully will soon draw uncertainties and risks.

Lord, I have no doubt that I love you, I believe in you, and I need you. I am convinced that you hear me and you are not indifferent to my problems. It is not your fault, but mine. Some days, as you know, having you so close to me, you are also so far. I feel a small rejection from you when you are far from me. I believe also that you are immutable, and, more or less, my tranquility in this convent matters to you. On other days, I don't believe in my life in the convent. It seems to me I chose wrong to accept it.

Sitting on the bed, she waits for the light of dawn that will guide her, and the one who wakes them begins to do so; despite all, it is a new day. When the sound of the troc-troc invades, Sister Edwina does not move and does not make the sign of the cross. In her navy blue suit, the outfit she wore when she entered the convent, she goes to the Reverend Mother to say goodbye.

"I am not a nun anymore. I will leave. Give me your blessing, please." Her voice breaks off. So much misery is in her that one is sorry for her!

"My child, are you not forgetting something?" she says with authority and disappointment.

They scrutinize each other with familiar eyes. What connects them is a loyalty curled up in a squall of memories, prospects, and hopes. What ties them together is the same love for their God. Their hearts are broken by the present suffering, and they are perplexed because they are entrapped by delusions and egoistic obligations and are incapable of reaching a solution with these impediments. They concede that the separation is near. They failed in something that cannot be seen. I am not sure for whom I have more pity. I want to think that it is for the younger, maybe because I feel that she is closer to me.

"No, Reverend Mother, I haven't forgotten anything," she says with solicitude and listlessness. Her voice is replete with whispering apprehensions.

"Yes, my child. Here you have your bride's dress. See the blood? It is yours. If the garment would stay here with us, then part of you is left behind," she declares with acrimony because it is as though the pin also punctured her skin. There is no blood, but the pain is real.

93

Sister Edwina can't find a suitable reply. A space of time that belongs only to her has been created. Nobody helps her. No human being can come to her aid. A world of spirals floats. The barriers, the dividers of everything, are joined and parted. Her gaze, lost in the existential voids, is probing the aridness and flabbiness of a nonsensical argument. Remembering something? Recalling the arrogance of an event with no beginning or end? Which fretful digressions are in this moment arising between a dying moon and a deceitfully tender sun? Which steps are audible in her inaccessible being? Is that yet the atmospheric time conspiring against her healthy state of intelligence, of the spiritual, and of the wish? Why is the Reverend Mother's questioning predictable but emotionless? Is it that something insentient or impassive is a portion of the creation by the nature of some type of an imperfect god who fabricates illusions, dreams, and even survivals? Yes, if it is like this, who is it, and where is it? My God, how very much alone we are! The strange current that we can rescue as tangible is the back and forth movement, in plea, of Sister Edwina Marie's eyes. They travel expanses impossible to be understood or valued. Time explodes in millions of insignificant and divided pieces. The Mother Superior is the only one to comprehend. It could as well be said that she feels it, but it is a dissimilar awareness, subdued, perhaps remote. Noticing by accident the countenance of the speaker, an incomparable peace relieves her. Do you recognize what just happened? I have the impression that the answer is yes.

"Reverend Mother, forgive me," she says, sobbing.

"My child, do not suffer. We are only travelers at the entrance to eternity." She manages a smile, but it is strained.

Sister Edwina falls to her knees. The Mother Superior goes to her and touches her head. Sister Edwina clutches her legs and weeps as she did as a child. The contact is fast and accepted.

The affirmation is confirmed but in some way, not established. There is a thrill of imperceptible variants and reasoning that is flawed. A contest of elusive probabilities that does not have logic has been instituted. Everything surges in a sea of bewilderments and challenges. From afar, a soft sound of a typewriter can be heard as a drizzle of doubts covers the place.

At the chapel, all the nuns attend the Mass celebrated by the elderly Father Blas. The Mother Superior and Sister Edwina Marie prepare to receive the Holy Communion.

Father Blas, recovered from his afflictions for some time now, is in his bedroom, illuminated by a weak light and secure in a late dawn. He walks to the desk chair, sits down, and starts to fill the blank page that accompanies him with weeks of reflections, oscillations, and trials.

He entitles his first novel *Looking for Sister Edwina Marie*.

Printed by Books on Demand GmbH, Norderstedt / Germany